ROMANCING THE WEIRD

C.D. WATSON

Bone Diggers Press
www.bonediggerspress.com

For B.

TABLE OF CONTENTS

INTRODUCTION

It's considered good form for an author to explain to readers how a certain short story collection came to be. I wish I could tell you the precise moment when I decided, "Oh, hey! I really want to write a bunch of Weird Romances and bundle them up in a short story collection."

If there was a moment like that, its memory eludes me now.

That's not to say that it wasn't lurking in the back of my mind, waiting to spring on me fully formed, only that I don't remember a moment of inception; there's nothing I can point to as the definitive conception for this collection other than the fact that, over time, I accumulated enough ideas for *Romancing the Weird* to be a real possibility.

Then there's the cover.

One day (I have no idea when, but almost certainly before I attended the RT Booklovers Convention in May 2017 in Atlanta), I was scrolling aimlessly through predesigned covers on a book cover design website when I spotted the perfect cover. That's the one you saw when you first picked this book up, physically or digitally. The cover was designed by Kristyn McQuiggen of Drop Dead Designs.

Have you ever had a moment where the heavens opened up and a ray of light shone down on you and you *just knew* something was exactly right? That's the kind of reaction I had when I saw Kristyn's cover, an epiphany. It was exactly what I was looking for, and it, as much as anything, helped cement *Romancing the Weird* into an actual collection.

As for the stories, they're equally as odd and fantastically astounding as the cover holding them together. The first two stories completed were, respectively, "Intersections" and "A Mutual Feeling," both of which were published independently as stand-alones in 2017.

"Intersections" was driven by an idea, yes, but also by a situation. It involved a man, as these things always do, and the infinite possibilities involved in courtship of any kind. My situation became the inspiration for Livy, who can see the future, but only when she's at a crossroads involving the man she's been dreaming of for her entire adult life.

"A Mutual Feeling" came about in a more straightforward manner. I woke up one day with a single line running through my head: "They came for Alice on a Wednesday morning." It took almost two years for me to finish writing what eventually became a quasi LitRPG with a definite Cyberpunk vibe, two years and about twenty thousand words. "A Mutual Feeling" is the longest story in this collection and also the first I started writing.

In many ways, "A Mutual Feeling" serves as the impetus behind the collection, if anything does. Once I get an idea, more ideas are sure to follow; like tribbles, ideas tend to multiply in my mind beyond control, filling up every available niche, nook, and cranny. At the time, however, it was just a cool premise about a video game character who thought she was real. I had no idea what I would do with the story once it was completed, nor did I care. The fun was in the exploration. I was quite content with that.

"Time after Time" is the only other of the included stories to have been published. This Time Travel Romance with a Steampunk feel was offered as an incentive to newsletter subscribers under one of my pen names, then placed on Wattpad where it remains freely available to anyone who wants to read it.

The idea for "Time after Time" came from a spontaneous brainstorming session with my son when we were out eating supper together one day. He said something like, "Wouldn't it be neat if two time travelers left notes to each other in books and fell in love?" With his permission, I adopted the idea and changed it to suit the needs of the enclosed story.

"Small Talk in Elevators" also exists thanks to my son's ingenious and wildly vivid imagination. We were standing in an elevator at the previously-mentioned RT Con, listening to people chatter with random strangers as they got on and off the elevator. When the elevator cleared, he leaned down to me and said, "What if...?" His idea was for a movie of such small talk; my take became an AI playing matchmaker with the humans in her care.

The remaining stories all had different inspirations.

"Our Song" developed after my editor and I attended a street festival in Greenville, South Carolina, where I witnessed an elderly couple dancing.

"A Lover's Kiss" was a thought experiment: What if Death fell in love? After some thought and a bit of puttering around, I ended up with a poignant tale deeply rooted in the need for companionship shared by every living creature. Oddly enough, this one has a libertarian core. Autonomy is also a basic need, but to explain any further would spoil the story.

"Brian" was the result of the coincidence of meeting several Brians who were all of a similar age, one right after the other.

"Tiny Moments" was derived from the intersection of reflections and lost loves. It, more than any of the others, follows Alice down the rabbit hole.

If you haven't figured it out already, the stories contained herein are a wide and varied mix of Fantasy, Science Fiction, and just plain Weird. All are Romances in one way or another, even "A Lover's Kiss," whose ending defies the traditional Happy Ever After.

The science in the SciFi stories should, however, be taken with a grain of salt. The emphasis for me, as I was writing each story, was on the characters, not on the technology. That said, aside from the time machine in "Time after Time," the technologies mentioned are at least plausible in the same way that everyone's good looking in a bar under dim lighting near closing time. The possibilities exist. We just haven't figured out all the details yet.

Several early readers told me that the stories have a very *Twilight Zone* feel, most notably Richard Parry (author of the Tyche Series) and *Romancing the Weird*'s narrator, Rebecca Winder. It's almost as if the characters are sliding down a wormhole leading to an unknown dimension and the reader is taken along for the ride.

I'm not sure anyone could've explained, or complimented, *Romancing the Weird* better than that.

TINY MOMENTS

Anna perched on the edge of a cushioned chair in front of the vanity, combing her hair. One stroke, two. The bristles were soft against her scalp, the silver handle cool in her grip. Her mind drifted into summer across possibilities, endless, tiny moments of sunshine and laughter and love.

He had been hers once. Her Charlie. That's what everyone said, and everyone would know, wouldn't they? They'd been inseparable that summer, moving in tandem across the halcyon landscape of weekend socials and weekday events so trivial and ordinary, even she had forgotten the details. Charlie had loved her once, in a perfect long ago, loved her more than she'd ever thought possible.

She shook out her hair and examined the golden curls reflected in the mirror. Age had failed to dull the color, though it had gifted her skin with crow's feet. Laugh lines, Charlie would've called them, but he was gone now and she'd never found another to supplant him.

A pang of loneliness tweaked her heart. She set the brush down and let memory slip away. It was better that way, best to move forward as she had more than three decades ago when she'd sat very much as she was now, on a chair in front of a mirror.

That mirror had been reality, reflecting a balmy autumn day as a wooden box empty of the physical remains of the only man she'd ever loved was lowered into the ground. For a moment, she was there again, surrounded by the soft cry of mourners and the sharp, metallic scent of fresh-turned earth. Sunshine warmed her hair, the tight clutch of her brother's arm around her shoulders comforted her, and the bleakness of Charlie's absence rested heavy within her heart.

Charlie was dead. She'd learned to live without him, though she'd never made peace with his death.

Anna rose abruptly and turned away from the mirror, heading for bed. Remembering wouldn't bring him back any more than love had. If it could, Charlie would never have left that day, no matter what had passed between them, no matter what either one of them had said, and she would never have spent one night alone, crying into the pillow that should've been his.

It was the same dream, always the same.

Charlie scrubbed a hand over his face, hiding sharp cheekbones and the dark shadows curving beneath amber colored eyes. "Anna, honey, stop. Where did you get a crazy idea like that?"

Anger and hurt swirled within her, carried on a swiftly flowing eddy. Her hands clenched into fists at her sides and her heart hammered against her chest. "I saw you, Charlie. I saw."

His hand dropped away from his face and his expression grew bleak. "I love *you*, Anna."

The doorbell chimed, shattering the dream like a stone tossed through glass. Anna's eyes popped open, and for a moment, Charlie stood superimposed against the chest of drawers, stalwart Charlie with his broad shoulders and cocksure grin, and enough patience to last a lifetime. Charlie as she'd last seen him, strong and bold and young, so very, very young.

The dream's last remnants faded under the hammer of a fist against the front door, and Charlie with it. Anna shoved the covers off her legs, and with it the bittersweet memories echoing in her mind.

"I'm coming," she called, and glanced at the time. Eight oh four, late for her, still a bit early for callers.

She raced down the stairs in bare feet, tugging a pink satin wrap over the matching nightgown as she went, and slung open the front door. Her nephew James stood on the stoop wearing a freshly pressed suit. A newspaper was tucked under his arm and in one hand, he held a bouquet of orange tulips wrapped in green tissue paper.

He clucked his tongue at her. "How many times have I warned you to see who's knocking before you open the door?"

"Not enough," she replied tartly. "Come in, darling. Let me get some water for those flowers."

"How do you know they're for you?"

Because he always brought them on the anniversary of Charlie's death. Because inside that tough exterior he exuded, James was a sensitive soul, and he loved his Aunt Anna.

And he knew how much she needed cheering, today of all days.

She stepped back and waited for him to enter, then closed the door behind him, shutting out the automatic sorrow rising within her along with the day's rising heat. "I'm the only woman in your life who loves orange tulips, that's how, so stop playing coy and give them over."

"You win," he murmured. He bent low and bussed her cheek, then handed her the tulips. "They're fresh from the flower stand downtown."

"Likely fresh from the farm, then. I've some freshly baked scones for you."

"And that's why you're my favorite aunt."

"I'm your only aunt," she retorted, but gently. "I'll fix you some chocolate milk—"

"I'm not five anymore!"

"In my heart, you'll always be five. Now, let me put these in water, then we can sit down and have a quick chat before you head off to work."

A few minutes later, the tulips were arranged in a leaded crystal vase gracing the center of the dinette situated in the sunroom off the kitchen, and Anna and James sat across from one another, him with a scone and a glass of chocolate milk. They chatted amiably for a while, mostly about his life. James worked at a bank across town, the headquarters of the one founded by Anna and his father's paternal grandfather. He'd started there as a teller the day after he turned eighteen and worked his way up to one of the vice president positions while attending college for this degree or that.

Charlie would've approved.

James carefully set his fork down, his dark eyes both astute and gentle. "You're thinking about him again."

"When am I not?" she said lightly.

"It's been decades."

She glanced away, focusing instead on the pattern of light streaming through the windows under the Kensington curtains hanging from rods at the head of each window frame. Yes, it had been decades since Charlie's death. That much she could aver.

"You have to let him go sometime," James continued.

"Must I?"

"I know you loved him, Anna." He sighed and sat back in his chair and dropped his napkin on the table beside his plate. "Ok, you win. Just promise me you won't brood about him all day. Get out and enjoy the sunshine. Come have lunch with me and Dad."

"All right, darling," she said, but they both knew she was humoring him. The day would unfold as it always did, steeped in memory and regret. Nothing she did could change that, or the past she'd unwittingly created.

James left a few minutes later. Anna cleaned up the small mess they'd made, then trudged upstairs and stepped into the shower. If the day had to be lived, the least she could do was be ready for it.

As soon as she was dressed, Anna headed out for a brisk walk, her purse and a light jacket slung over her forearm. Breakfast had gone by the wayside, nudged aside by the urgency filling her to move, to breathe, to stand in the sunlight and remember what it was like to be alive.

Her footsteps lead her inevitably to the park, and while she'd known deep in her heart exactly where they would carry her, she was still surprised to arrive there.

Not much had changed in the three and a half decades since Charlie's untimely death. There was the oak they'd sat under during those first heady days of discovery, after they'd met, its branches coated in autumn's colors. There was the gazebo where he'd proposed. The roses growing up its latticework had been replaced, of course; some had simply died out over time, but aside from minor changes in color and form, the view was the same. The swings had been taken down. Naturally, as they'd been metal and twenty feet tall at least, and had posed a safety risk with their long, rusty chains and tenuous, plastic seats.

But the lake, that hadn't changed one bit.

A family of ducks swam there now, along the edges near the rushes and cattails. A weathered dock gleamed silver under the early October sun. Water lapped along its pilings, driven there by the wake of a fishing boat bobbing along the far side. The road that had once skirted the edges was gone now, replaced by a walking path lined with a sturdy wooden fence standing between it and the water. Anna's father had petitioned the city to make those changes, after the incident.

That was what he'd always called Charlie's death. *The incident,* as if a minor inconvenience had occurred. As if a man hadn't died at the whim of a young, headstrong girl torn between the throes of first love and jealousy.

They'd never found his body, only the car that had carried him to his watery death.

She found herself on the dock, her sandal clad toes aligned with its edge. The water was brown here, murky. Sunlight bounced off its surface, creating a perfect mirror behind which fish swam among the long fronds of weeds littering the lake's sandy bottom.

Charlie's face was reflected there, smiling up at her, and without thinking, Anna knelt and bent over and touched a single finger to his cheek.

The water rippled outward from her intrusion, breaking the mirrored surface, and Charlie's image shatter into disjointed pieces carried off in the waves.

"Oh, Charlie," she said, her voice a shallow tremble, and she knelt there for a long while, pinned by the memories wafting over her, carried by the breeze.

To appease James's worry, Anna caught a taxi outside the park, when she could finally pry herself away from the memories, and had it take her to the bank, just before James and her brother would leave there for their weekly lunch date.

And regretted every second spent with her less than sensitive sibling. Thank God James had inherited his mother's compassion along with his father's business sense.

After, she strolled along the sidewalks, window shopping until her feet reminded her that she wasn't used to so much walking. She caught a cab home, carried the small purchases she'd made inside, and allowed herself a single, hand-crafted truffle with her afternoon tea, then changed into her gardening clothes and fell asleep in the hammock stretched between two stalwart oaks in her back yard.

And dreamed of Charlie.

"I love *you*, Anna," he insisted, his hands cupping her cheeks. "We're supposed to get married and have babies and grow old together."

Anna jerked away from him, sniffing back the tears she refused to hide. "And I'm supposed to accept your mistresses, is that it? Accept them the way my mother did my father's affairs?"

His hands were on his hips now, and he was cold, so cold and distant. His image wavered in her mind and his voice dimmed. "There's nobody but you. Why won't you believe me?"

A hand fell on her shoulder, startling her, and her eyes popped open on a gasp. James stood beside her, his expression creased into worry, and for the tiniest moment, Charlie's face was reflected there, as it had been at the lake.

Anna rubbed her eyes, scrubbing the dream from her foggy mind, though not from her wounded heart. No, Charlie was dead. How many times did she have to tell herself that before she believed it?

"You ok?" James asked.

"I'm fine, dear." Anna dropped her hand and placed it in his, and struggled up and out of the hammock. "Just a late afternoon nap. Old woman that I am, I needed one."

James snorted. "You're barely fifty, hardly old."

"I'm fifty-two and that's old enough." She finally managed to place her feet on terra firma and stand unassisted, then glanced up and squinted her eyes against the sun's halo surrounding his handsome head. "What's wrong?"

"Nothing. I thought we could have supper together, maybe catch a movie."

"Weren't two meals together today enough?"

His mouth firmed into a narrow slash across his face and his hand tightened on hers. "I'm worried about you."

"There's nothing wrong with me, other than too much walking."

"No," he insisted. "Something's going on. There's something different about you today."

Charlie's face popped into her head, the way it always did on this day above all others, but she shook it away and said gently, "I'm fine, truly."

"Are you sure?"

"Positive. Now, about that movie."

James's expression cleared and he grinned down at her. "There's a new Stephen King flick playing."

She groaned and protested that she'd have nightmares, but in the end, she let James talk her into dinner and a movie. After he dropped her back off at home that night, she was so exhausted, she fell straight to sleep, and if she dreamed of Charlie, the remnants of it were lost by the time she woke the next morning.

The next few days passed uneventfully, and Anna gradually settled back into the routine the anniversary of Charlie's death had disrupted. Her days were spent volunteering at the hospital her grandfather had helped build and to various literacy causes. She especially loved working with young children, and so, spent as much time in the pediatric ward as possible.

Her nights were a whirlwind of fundraisers and community meetings, and planning for the same. It was fulfilling work, a way for her family to give back to the people who'd supported the bank for so long, either through trusting it with their money, or by investing in it.

One rainy day, she sat in her home office steadily working her way through a pile of invitations and correspondence. The doorbell rang, interrupting her in the middle of deciding whether or not to speak at the Rotary Club. She marked the email unread and closed out the email provider, then walked through the house and opened the door.

And wished she'd taken the time to check who was on the other side, as James so often insisted she should.

A woman a few years Anna's junior stood there, wearing a sleek, black pants suit under a brilliant red overcoat. Her hair was a cap of well-tamed bronze curls, the same color as the braids a younger version of this same woman had worn when she was much younger, and her amber colored eyes were the exact shade of her brother's.

Anna's heart sank and she struggled to maintain her composure. Charlie's sister. Of all people to show up on her door.

"Anna," Janine said, ending the single word on a questioning lilt.

Her voice opened a flood of memories in Anna's mind, of sunshine and laughter and friendship, and a tremulous breath whispered out of her. She shook the memories away and stepped back, opening the door wider. "Won't you come in?"

Janine stepped carefully across the threshold and into the foyer. "I hope I'm not bothering you."

Anna shut the door, then folded her hands together in front of her. "Not at all. Would you like some tea, or perhaps some hot chocolate?"

"No. I just..." Janine's hands shot out and latched onto Anna's forearms. Her palms were cold, much colder than the weather warranted, and her face went ashen beneath a light dusting of powder. "I wasn't sure if I should come or not, but I finally had to."

"You were always welcome," Anna said gently, and clasped Janine's hands in her own. If circumstances had been different, this woman would've been her sister, or the next best thing to it, and there would never have been a question as to her place in Anna's home. "Let's sit down and have that tea, shall we?"

"Hot chocolate," Janine murmured. "For old times' sake. Have you been dreaming about Charlie?"

The question took Anna aback. She paused in the middle of turning toward the kitchen and glanced at Janine. "I always do around this time of year. Why?"

"I have been, and it's..." Janine's mouth pinched shut and her expression contorted into pain. "It's almost like he's still here with us, or just beyond my reach."

"I know. I feel him, too."

"They never found his body."

Anna shrugged, more to ease the pain of his loss than anything. "But we all know he drowned in that lake."

"Did he?"

"Of course. What else could've happened? If he'd lived through the crash, he would've found help. He would've—"

"Come back to us?" Janine shook her head. "I've been seeing his reflection everywhere, in my bathroom mirror, in plate glass windows of stores I walk past, in the lake."

Anna froze and her hands went stiff on Janine's, and when she spoke, her voice was a hoarse whisper. "Me, too."

They stood there looking at each other for long, long moments, each trapped in the past's endless realm of mistakes and possibilities. Finally, Janine said, "Maybe we need something stronger than hot chocolate."

"I've just the thing," Anna said.

They sat for a long time at the dinette, watching the afternoon fade into night as they sipped hot chocolate laced with Kahlúa and talked of Charlie and the life he'd lived, of their love for him and the laughter, and of the day he died and his sudden, odd reappearance in their lives, however imaginary.

"It has to be our imaginations," Janine said. "What else could it be?"

"But for both of us to see him, and in the same way?" Anna shook her head, sending blonde curls bouncing over her shoulders and the tailored blouse she wore. "How can we be sharing a delusion, when we haven't spoken to each other in years?"

"Decades," Janine murmured. "I should never have stayed away so long."

"It takes two to make or break a friendship, darling."

"Then we should both have tried harder."

They should've. On that, Anna could fully agree. "Now that we've had our aperitif, perhaps we should eat."

"Oh, I've imposed enough for one day."

Anna reached across the table and placed her hand on Janine's. "You're never an imposition. Stay. We'll order in, something horribly fattening and delicious. We can watch a movie and pretend we're teen-agers."

"No pillow fights. You always won."

"Because I always cheated."

Janine laughed and turned her hand over in Anna's, meeting it palm to palm, and her eyes sparkled exactly as Charlie's used to when he was happy. "You can't cheat at pillow fights."

"Little do you know," Anna said, laughing, and then she hunted out menus and they called in an order, and spent the rest of the evening indulging in fattening food, excellent wine, and the companionship they'd forsaken after their Charlie had died.

They fell asleep in the TV room, shoulder to shoulder on the sofa as they had so often when they were teenagers. Then, the movies were made for the small screen or had long since ended their run on the big screen. A different world, made the same by the friendship they'd renewed that night.

A hint of something familiar woke Anna. She shifted on the sofa, felt the weight of her friend against her, and remembered, and in the remembering, smiled.

"Anna," someone whispered, and she glanced up.

Charlie was on the TV, his image superimposed against a black screen and the reminder her digital streaming service popped up when the user hadn't interacted with it for a while.

Anna placed her fingertips against her forehead. Too much wine. That's what she got for splitting an entire bottle with Janine, then opening a second one. She eyed the empty bottles sitting on the coffee table and cursed the headache she'd have come morning.

"Come on, Anna," Charlie said. "Talk to me."

"You're not real," she said, then winced. Of course, he wasn't real; he was a product of her grief and too much vino, and since he was, she shouldn't be talking to him.

"I missed you."

"Well, I missed you, too," she hissed. "But I'm going to wake Janine now and get her in bed, then I'm going to bed myself."

"I'll help."

She glanced sharply at the TV and the image wavering there, somewhat less solid than it had been a moment before. "Go away."

His smile slowly faded and his expression turned serious, then he turned and walked away. His image became smaller and smaller, until finally, he was no larger than the lettering he had walked into, and he disappeared.

"Oh, my God," Janine said. "Tell me that was a dream."

Anna slumped into the sofa. "I don't know what that was."

"You saw it, too?"

"Yes. He...spoke to me."

Janine shifted around, facing Anna. Her hair and clothes were rumpled and a faint crease line married her finely boned cheek. "What did he say?"

"He missed me."

"That's it?"

Anna replayed what she could remember of the conversation already blurring in her mind. "That was the important part."

"What's going on here, Anna?"

"I don't know," Anna murmured. "I just don't know."

They sat for a moment in silence, then went upstairs together and brushed their teeth, one after the other, and climbed into their respective beds, Janine in the guest room down the hall. For a long while, Anna lay in hers listening to the wind and rain whispering to one another outside her window, wondering about the state of her sanity, and Janine's.

Janine left early the next morning, citing a busy schedule and family. They made plans for a lunch date the following week and promised to keep in touch, and after, Anna spent the day finishing the correspondence she'd forsaken the previous afternoon in favor of the company of Charlie's sister.

Whenever she passed a mirror or another reflective surface, she averted her gaze, almost afraid of hallucinating again.

Perhaps she should see someone. A psychiatrist or a counselor. Her mother had tried to coax her into therapy after Charlie's funeral, but Anna had refused to go, and her father had refused to make her.

On impulse, Anna packed a picnic and drove to the lake. She spread an old blanket out along the dock and slowly ate a sandwich, and watched the clouds drift across autumn's blue sky.

And still, she couldn't bring herself to look into the water, for fear of what she'd find, or what she wouldn't, but she felt better sitting there listening to the ducks quacking and the water lap against the dock's pilings. She felt connected to Charlie, the way she always had, and unbidden, memory intruded on her interlude.

"Why won't you believe me?" Charlie said.

Anna's hands balled up into fists by her side. "I saw you kissing her."

Charlie huffed out a breath. "You saw me saying goodbye."

"Is that what you call a kiss now? What about sex? Is that just a hello?"

"Don't be ridiculous, Anna."

"I'm not!"

He leveled a hard gaze on her. "My parents told me I needed to let you grow up some. I told them no, you're seventeen, old enough to know your own mind, mature enough to handle a real relationship. I guess I was wrong."

His words sliced right through her, wounding her to the core. She gasped and said, her voice furiously twisted, "Well, maybe I was a fool to trust you, Charlie Danforth, and since I was, you can just leave now, leave and never come back."

His hands dropped to his sides and his expression flattened into a hard mask. "If that's what you want, ok."

She screamed at him then, venting her fury and hurt into the air between them. The least he could do was argue with her, fight for her, do something other than fall into that placid calm he used as a shield against her. "I hate you, Charlie. I hate everything about you."

He blinked at her once, then calmly turned and walked away, and he never looked back.

An engine's roar startled Anna out of the past, and she glanced around, confused. She was kneeling on the edge of the dock, one hand held there, steadying her, and the other stretched toward the water and

Charlie's reflection.

"It's ok, Anna," he said. "Come with me. I've been waiting for you."

A hand touched her shoulder, startling her, and she jerked her arm back and twisted around and glanced up into the concerned face of the woman standing beside her.

"You ok, ma'am?" the woman asked.

Anna nodded and scrambled to her feet, careful to keep her gaze away from the water as her heart boomed in her chest and fear settled into a greasy knot in her stomach. "I thought I saw something."

"In the water?"

"Yes. Sorry." Anna shook her head and forced a laugh. "A piece of trash, I'm sure. It's gone now."

The woman's expression cleared and she grimaced through a sympathetic smile. "Yeah, these kids. They don't know how to clean up after themselves, do they?"

"They'll learn," Anna said, then she exchanged goodbyes with the woman and gathered her things with trembling hands, and forced herself to walk calmly and slowly back to her car in spite of the emotions weakening her limbs.

Anna told no one of the incident, not even Janine, though she was sorely tempted at least half a dozen times over the next few days. What could she say? No one would believe the truth, if she could even sort out what truth lay before her.

Perhaps Charlie's death had finally carved away the last remnants of her sanity, or perhaps her guilt had finally done her in.

She cancelled her appointments and appearances, and wandered down the long, narrow hallways of her grandfather's home, pondering recent events. Searching for answers, though they eluded her. What little comfort she found within the walls of her childhood home was lost each time she passed a mirror.

God forbid she see him again.

What had he meant, that day at the lake? *Come with me. I've been waiting for you.*

Anna shook her head and scraped her fingernails against the wainscoating in what had once been her grandfather's study, and would've been Charlie's. "He's not real," she reminded herself in a stark whisper. "He can't be real."

That night, she forsook her usual bedtime routine and went to bed without brushing her hair. She couldn't sit in front of the vanity and risk seeing him again. One more appearance and she would be forced to call a psychologist, at the very least. One more time and she'd go mad.

Her dreams were blessedly free of Charlie's apparition. She was drawn instead into a murky nightmare centered on his funeral and the empty wooden coffin, its satin interior glinting in a single ray of sunshine as the Reverend intoned Psalms 23:4.

Yea though I walk through the valley of the shadow of death.

I didn't, Charlie whispered, and the words echoed and folded into themselves, swirling into a tunnel leading directly to the lake. *Come be with me.*

Water lapped at her feet. She wiggled her toes in mud, and it sucked her in, pulling her down. An arm wrapped itself around her waist and heaved her backward, and she woke on a scream, sitting upright in bed, the feel of Charlie's body against hers so fresh, her heart contracted in her chest and tears clouded her vision.

"I fought it, too, you know," he said.

She glanced up and gasped. Charlie's transparent image was superimposed against the chest of drawers beside her, reflected in its gloss. Her heart leapt into her throat and she scrambled away from him, back, back, until her feet touched the opposite side of the bed.

"What do you want from me?" she asked.

"Never fear." He held out a hand, and his expression held such remorse, she almost went to him. "I still love you, Anna. So much. It's been hell living without you."

"I know." She shook her head, bringing herself back to reality, to this place and this time and this moment, and she pressed her palm against her heart, as a reminder of what that reality was. Her, alone. Always. "You're not real."

"What's real, honey? Do I feel real? Do I look real?" His hand dropped to his side and he frowned. "I thought you'd be ready, once I found a way. I thought you'd want to be with me again."

"I did, more than anything. Oh, Charlie." A sigh shuddered out of her and she sniffed back the tears. "I wish I'd believed you that day, and I wish to God I'd never pushed you away."

"It's ok."

"No! I killed you with my childish, petty jealousy, and I can never make that right."

"You can, if you'll just trust me." He held his hand out again and his expression was calm, sure. "Take my hand, Anna. Take it and be with me."

Her fingers twitched reflexively against her skin, above the lace edge of her nightgown. "I can't."

The doorbell rang, slicing through their interlude, and Anna glanced at the clock. Almost 9:30 and she hadn't even showered yet. How long had she been tangled up in dream and memory and regret?

"That was always your problem, Anna," Charlie said, his voice thin and distant and fading. "You never trusted me."

"I did, Charlie, I—"

She looked at the space where he'd been, but the gloss was merely polish now and the chest of drawers no longer reflected the man she'd loved so long ago. Regret slumped her shoulders and she rubbed her eyes with trembling fingers. A psychologist it was, then, else James would end up committing her, if his father didn't beat him to the punch.

James was at the door. Anna peeked through the security port for once and saw him standing patiently on her stoop, and almost left him there.

But he was her nephew, beloved above all others, save Charlie, and she needed him now.

She opened the door without bothering to smooth her hair or tidy the robe she'd thrown on over her nightgown.

James took one look at her and frowned. "You're sick."

She shook her head, pressed a clammy palm to her forehead. "No, darling. I'm not sleeping well."

James stepped inside and closed the door on the wind rattling leaves across the front lawn. "Charlie?"

"Yes," she said, and everything poured out of her then, the apparitions, his reflection wherever she went, him asking her to come with him, almost falling into the lake, everything she could remember exactly as it had happened.

When she wound down and stood there in her bare feet with her hands wrung into a knot in front of her, James pulled her into a hug and held her close. "Let me make you some breakfast while you shower and put on some fresh clothes."

Shame washed over her then, staining her cheeks, and she nodded against his chest. This was what her broken heart had reduced her to, the status of a child in need of another's care.

How had she come to this?

Meekly, she climbed the stairs to her bedroom, showered and changed into jeans and a light sweater, and came downstairs to the kitchen. James was standing at the stove wearing an apron over his slacks and dress shirt. The sleeves were rolled up to mid-forearm and his suit jacket and tie were draped over a dinette chair.

She smiled and leaned a hip against the counter near him. "You always loved to cook."

"Dad nearly forbade it until you stepped in and told him—"

"Everyone should be able to feed himself," she murmured. "I'm fine, you know, or will be."

James's mouth thinned into a line as he forked bacon out of a pan onto a plate topped with paper towels. At last, he said, "There's a place on Bedford Drive overlooking the lake. It's beautiful there. Peaceful. The staff is kind and very professional."

She gaped at him, then slowly closed her mouth. "You want to have me committed."

He set the pan off the eye and said, gently, "You're suicidal, Anna."

"No! Of course not." She shook her head and laughed, a sad, little sputtering sound lacking all but the faintest trace of humor. Hadn't she been worried about exactly this? Loony Anna, driven 'round the bend by the love of a dead fiancé? "I'm not suicidal, James. That's what's so puzzling about all this."

"But you hear him calling to you, asking you to drown yourself, or step into a reflection, or—"

"Or be with him," Anna said. "I know how it sounds."

"Do you?" James huffed out a laugh, then cracked eggs into the pan and returned it to the eye. "You know I love you."

"Of course, darling. I love you, too, very much."

"Then let me help you. Don't make me watch you spiral away from us into some dark hole where we can't find you anymore."

Touched, she placed a hand on his forearm and squeezed gently. "Give me a few more days to sort it out on my own."

"And then?"

She shrugged and let her hand slide away from him. "Then I'll seek professional help."

He glanced at her out of the corners of his eyes, his mouth twisted into a skeptical frown. "Promise?"

"On my honor," she vowed, and she fully intended to, as soon as she set her affairs in order.

They ate breakfast together, a late one for both of them, then James rushed off to work and Anna headed toward her study. The first thing she did was make an appointment with her lawyer for early the next morning to go over her will. James was her primary beneficiary, along with a handful of her favorite charities. That had always been the case, but she wanted to make absolutely certain the will itself was ironclad. It would be just like her brother to try to contest it should something happen to her, and damned if she wanted him to touch a red cent of the money and property she'd inherited from their father.

After, she visited the hospital and spent some time in the children's ward, reading books or playing games with its residents, chatting with the parents who could afford to take time off to stay with their sick children.

Soon, her day was done, her time her own, and a long evening loomed ahead of her. She parked her car in the massive garage attached to her house and walked to the park, stood on the dock well back from its edge and stared over the lake, her arms wrapped around herself, warding off the wind's chill.

And thought of Charlie.

He'd lingered in her thoughts for so long, decades now, she hardly knew how to function without him there. No more. It was past time to let him go, to move on with her life, to fully live again. He would never have wanted her to pine away for him, or to hide herself from the world as she'd been doing, burying herself in charitable work so she would never have to love again.

There's another option, her mind whispered, but she shoved that aside and walked home under the darkening sky, forcing her thoughts onto what she could order for supper instead.

Charlie was waiting for her in the massive mirror mounted to a wall in the foyer. "You were gone a long time," he said quietly.

She shut the door behind herself, locked it tight, and resigned herself to the inevitable. Until she found help, Charlie was going to seem real to her. She might as well treat him that way. "I walked to the lake and back."

He glanced away and down, then back to her. "We used to do that all the time."

"Long ago, when we were young and you were—"
Alive.

She bit the word off, attempted a tremulous smile. "I was about to order a pizza."

His expression cleared and he laughed. "I thought you hated pizza. Too undignified, too common."

"I've grown up," she said lightly. "Into a woman who loves her pie."

"I like this woman."

She laughed then and touched a single fingertip to his reflection. To her surprise, the mirror flexed slightly and a deep, penetrating cold coated her finger. She yanked her hand away and instinctively stuck the wounded digit in her mouth, and her eyes were wide and wary.

"I should've warned you about that," he said.

"The cold?"

"The mirror." He shrugged and seemed to struggle with something, then finally said, "It takes some getting used to."

Oh, of that she had no doubt. "Why now?"

"It took me a while to figure out what I was, how to find you. I had to gather enough strength to bring you through."

She nodded, though she didn't really understand. "What are you?"

"The man who loves you," he said simply, and his image began to fade. "Tomorrow?"

Startled, she said, "Yes." A moment later, the mirror reflected only her, wide-eyed, ashen Anna, golden curls scattered around her shoulders, the way they'd been when she was young and free.

For a moment, her reflection was that impetuous, headstrong teenager, grinning back at her through three and half decades of time. Then Anna blinked and her image shimmered and became her as she was now, and the weight of those years crashed down around her, aging her in an instant.

She touched a tentative finger to the silvered glass, found it firm and ungiving, and shook her head. Her delusions certainly were detailed, she'd give them that, but enough pondering the past, she decided. Nothing else was going to get between her and that pizza she'd promised herself.

Anna dreamed that night not of Charlie, but of Janine, of an open grave and an empty casket, of angry tears and recriminations, and of the hearts broken by the loss of a beautiful soul.

She woke in the pre-dawn morning with sunlight only just filtering through the curtains in her bedroom, lighting the room by slow and shallow increments. One glance around and she knew she was alone. Charlie wasn't there, waiting in the mirror or a reflection cast along another surface. Maybe he never had been. Perhaps he was only alive in her imagination, and Janine's.

No, that wasn't quite right, or if it was, she was as delusional and in need of help as James thought her to be.

She slid out of bed and gathered fresh clothes. Today, a cleaning crew would come in and spruce the house up from top to bottom, a weekly routine she usually relished overseeing. Not today. Today would be for answers and certainty, for clarifying Charlie's realness, or not. Today was for preparations, just in case.

Later, she promised herself, after her appointment with her attorney and the cleaning crew's departure.

She was waiting in the foyer when the cleaning crew arrived, and left them there with the promise of returning before they'd finished for a good bout of gossip. She drove straight downtown to her lawyer's firm through a cold October rain, sat in the discreetly appointed waiting room flipping through an architectural magazine until he could see her.

The meeting went smoothly. Yes, her will was solid and unimpeachable. No one could break it. Did she need to make changes of any kind?

Anna said no and gave him the letters she'd written the previous night after her pizza fest, along with strict instructions as to when and why to deliver them. She shook her attorney's hand and thanked him for his time, and since she was so close to the bank, she stopped in and said hello to her beloved nephew, carefully avoiding discussion of Charlie or anything related to him.

What a shame, to have to hide such lovely encounters.

If they were real.

A few errands later, she headed for home. The rain had intensified, forestalling a trip to the park, but her cleaning crew was still at her home, as she'd expected them to be. She took a moment to greet each member properly and ask after family, then retreated to her office and sat staring out the window at the gray day, her mind blessedly empty of all but the simplest thoughts.

What if she could follow Charlie, not into death, but into whatever reality had captured him when his car had crashed into the lake?

The cleaning crew's leader knocked on her office door mid-afternoon and informed Anna that they were finished unless she had any further work. She smiled and said no and handed off a check with a hefty bonus, pretending that all was as it usually was.

But in her heart, everything was changing, changing and growing and wondering, and she wasn't quite sure what to make of it all.

* * *

That night, Anna sat at her vanity, slowly brushing her hair. The brush's silver handle glinted in the light cast by the bedside lamp and reflected in the mirror. She set the brush down, ran her fingers through her hair, then folded her hands in her lap and stared at her own reflection.

"Where are you, Charlie?" she murmured.

Slowly, his image appeared, as if he stood behind her. The illusion was so real, she could almost feel the heat shimmering off his skin through the t-shirt he wore.

The same t-shirt he'd worn on that fateful day when he'd left her standing in front of her family's home and walked away forever.

She crossed her arms together over her chest and placed her hands on her shoulders, expecting him to touch her has he used to, to rest his hands on hers, to bend and kiss her cheek.

His image remained still, unwavering. "Hello, Anna. You've had a long day."

"Yes." She sighed and let her hands drop into her lap. "It's been busy."

"Something's bothering you."

"I'm seeing visions of my long-lost fiancé," she said lightly. "Shouldn't that bother me?"

"At least you're not being sarcastic."

"I outgrew that a long time ago."

He smiled at her then, a faint stretch of his lips that didn't quite touch his eyes. She wanted so badly to turn around and find him there, to bury her face in his stomach and have his arms around her once again, but she remained as she was, staring at what was left of him. If she turned around, he'd disappear, leaving her alone once again with memories she'd rather not endure.

"I'm so tired, Charlie." The words tumbled out of her of their own free will, pushed out by some feeling she had yet to name. "I'm tired of remembering and tired of dreaming about you. I'm tired of knowing I'll never have you."

A sobbing hiccup interrupted the rush of words, bringing them to a stumbling halt. She blinked away the tears, felt them roll down her cheeks, and Charlie was in front of her in the mirror now, his hand stretched toward her.

"I'm sorry, sweetheart," he murmured. "I wish you were here so I could touch you. If you'd just trust me for once, we could be together again."

"Oh, Charlie."

On impulse, she raised her own hand and reached out to him, and to her utter shock and surprise, her fingers touched his a foot in front of the mirror. They were cold and slick, like the mirror itself, not at all as she remembered him being.

His laugh was half surprise, half disbelief. "You're touching me. God, Anna. I've missed feeling you. Can I...?"

He didn't wait for an answer, merely opened his hand and pressed it against her palm. His skin was warmer now, less smooth, more like flesh than mirror. He bent and placed his lips to the back of her hand, and she realized his head was a mere two feet from her own, so close, the scent of his shampoo tickled her nose.

But he wasn't real, was he? How then could she smell something so distinctive, other than memory getting the better of her? How could she feel him if he wasn't real?

"Anna," he whispered against her skin. "Come with me."

Tentatively, she reached out with her other hand and touched a lock of his hair. It was soft under her fingertips, silky as it had always been. She curled her fingers into it and tugged gently, and when he lifted his face to hers, leaned forward and touched her lips to his, kissing him for the first time in decades.

Clarity struck so sharply, she gasped against his mouth. What did it matter if he was real or not? He was here and he loved her, and he could be hers again, if she only believed.

She broke the kiss abruptly, intending to tell him so, but it was already too late. The world whirled around her, flashing through a light so silvery bright, it blinded her and stole her breath, and through it all, Charlie surrounded her, holding her to him as she slipped from her world into his.

She passed out for a time, and when she woke, he was looking down at her in a mirror image of her bedroom.

He stroked her hair back and slid his fingers through her curls. "You ok?"

"I don't know. Am I really…is this real?"

"It's as real as we need it to be." His arm tightened against her back, lifting her to him, and he brushed the tip of his nose against hers. "There's no going back now, Anna. I know. I tried for years."

"It's ok, Charlie. I want to be here."

"Are you sure?"

She thought of the long decades without him, of her conversations with James and Janine, of the letters she'd written to them and left with her attorney, and the love that had never fully faded from her heart. "I've never been more sure of anything in my life. There's just one problem."

"Yeah?"

"You haven't aged a day in the past three and a half decades, whereas I—"

"Whereas you," he said gently, "are still the most beautiful woman I've ever known. Close your eyes."

She did as he asked, trusting him as she should've so long ago, and when he asked her to, opened them again and found a much older version of him staring down at her. Laughter sputtered out of her and she cupped his face in hers. "How did you do that?"

"Anything's possible here, my love. Anything and everything, now that I have you."

"Show me," she said, and he pulled her to her feet and kissed her, and showed her everything she needed to know about her place in his heart.

OUR SONG

Liberty hung in the metal carapace holding her aging body upright. Wires and tubes erupted from the frame's rear girders: Feeding tubes, a catheter, supplemental oxygen, everything needed to sustain the shell she'd become.

Her mind was still sharp, sharp as ever, really, and that was the important thing.

I reached up and gently unlatched the plate covering her face, waited while the respirator supporting her lungs adjusted to the room's perfect mixture of air. She'd been on it for too long, and that was my fault.

Well, not the reason she was on it; that had nothing to do with me. But the wait while I scraped together the funds to repair her damaged body, working three and four jobs at a time, applying for every grant I could find, and applying again when we were rejected through an innocent oversight of some bureaucratic technicality. Living a pauper's life so I could pay for her care, saving the smallest credit for her.

It had taken years, and in that time, the technology had changed. Gotten better, sure, but gotten cheaper, too, and then finally, something new had come along, something only dreamed of in the wildest Science Fiction stories I'd read as a kid.

The respirator finished whirring (damned PoS outdated tech, the best we could afford), the faceplate popped off. I pulled it out of the way, careful not to twist it into her fragile face, and at last, there she was, my darling Liberty.

We'd met at a street fair in our hometown, back before flying cars and the Mars colony, back when meeting was done through an app on your phone, not through a genetic facility's matchmaking services like kids did nowadays.

The ultimate compatibility, those centers promised, but it was the government, and when the government promises something, you'd better run the other way.

I shook my head as I laughed at myself. A fool and his stories of the good ol' days, eh?

We were young then, her a freshman in college, me a brash developer on the verge of changing the world (so I told myself). Bumped into each other in the middle of town, and I'd looked into her soft green eyes, fallen into her laughter, and that was it for me.

Took me a while to convince her, of course. Smart woman, my Libby, but she gave in eventually, through my puppy dog persistence or because she'd fallen in love, or maybe both. She'd played that one close to her chest until I'd asked her to be mine forever, and she'd agreed on one condition: That I'd be hers forever, too.

And we had been.

The nurse-technician came around the carapace and helped me unhook the torso plates, limb supports, and interior restraints, the bands holding her into the carapace. She slid out of it into my arms, and I stumbled back, surprised by her weight. It had been so long since I'd held her, even longer since the accident that had severed her spinal cord and paralyzed her from the neck down.

Drunk driver. Late night. Rain slicked road. Liberty had been coming home from a girls' night out. The accident report was clear. She'd been in her lane going a little under the speed limit. The other driver had nodded off, lost control of her vehicle, and swerved into Liberty's lane. Liberty had yanked the steering wheel a little too hard, gone into a spiraling fishtail helped along by the other car kissing her bumper, and skidded off the road into a tree.

The crash had woken the other driver. She managed to stop her car, then called emergency services. To her credit, she'd waited beside Liberty until an ambulance arrived. They'd arrested her on the scene. She'd served some time, found Jesus, sobered up. Led AA meetings in her local church every night until she died of a heart attack half a decade back.

Every Sunday after she got out of prison, she brought flowers to Liberty, every single one. I guess that was her way of atoning for what she'd done. I never asked. Never spoke to the woman unless I had to. Liberty had, though, until her own heart had failed and we'd had to put her in the carapace just to keep her alive while I scraped up the money to have her spinal cord repaired.

The nurse-technician (new one this week, what was his name again?) finished unhooking the tubes and whatnot from Liberty while I stood there trembling with my arms wrapped tight around her and my face buried in her hair. It smelled like orange blossoms, her favorite.

The scent carried me back to the first time we'd danced. Our first date. I'd taken her to the county fair, and there surrounded by the aroma of funnel cakes and dust and cattle, I'd held her hand in mine and led her out onto the hardwood floor, and we'd two-stepped under a gibbous moon held up by a million stars.

She'd looked up at me and said, real solemn, "They're playing our song."

I'd looked down and smiled, and me being a man and all, I'd said the dumbest thing. "We don't have a song."

She'd broken into that grin of hers and squeezed my hand. "We do now."

And that had been the end of that. We'd danced to the same song on our wedding day. "Baby, I'm in Love with You." Truth be told, I hadn't been in love with her that night, but it hadn't taken me long to fall and I'd loved her ever since.

I'd never thought I could love anybody as much as I loved her, or that this old man had it in him to love somebody for so long.

The nurse-technician cupped a bear-sized hand over my shoulder. "You ready now, Mr. McKenzie?"

"The song," I said.

He grinned at me and snapped his fingers. "Knew I was forgetting something. Just a minute."

He hustled away, fast now because Liberty really only had a few moments before her organs shut down without the support of all those machines. She was already wheezing for breath. Hurry, hurry, no time to waste now.

Then scratchy music filled the air, and I smiled and shuffled me and her both into a two-step as Ricky Skaggs sang and the nurse-technician returned and gently guided us toward the waiting pod.

"Our last dance, Lib," I whispered to her. "One last dance in this body. I've got a new one for you, brand spanking new. You're gonna love it, just you wait and see."

The nurse-technician picked Liberty up, breaking my shaky hold on her, and tucked her into the pod, and began hooking up all the do-dads that would help transfer her consciousness to the force-grown clone waiting patiently in another pod.

I leaned over and kissed her forehead. "Don't worry, Lib. This won't hurt a bit."

Her eyes cut to mine, those soft green eyes, and her lips trembled into a smile, and in my mind, I heard her say what she no longer had the breath to speak.

They're playing our song, Jim.

Yes, they were, and someday soon, we'd dance to it again, the way we had the first night we'd danced.

I stepped out of the way and settled into a chair in the corner of the white, sterile room, and waited for Liberty to come back to me while the computer looped around and played our song again.

BRIAN

A sporty red Miata occupied the space where Madison usually parked.

She tightened her two-handed grip on the steering wheel and stared at the offending vehicle as the radio blared a pop song she hated and snow drifted down around her car. This was her parking spot. Sure, the lot had no assigned parking, but everybody knew where everybody else parked, and nobody ever violated that unspoken rule.

It was like passing in line or chewing with your mouth open at a dinner party: Just plain rude.

She heaved a long-suffering sigh, backed up. Executed a nifty k-turn and found a spot not claimed by anyone else. It was closer to the entrance, but so what? Her spot was hers. She'd parked there since she started at Hinkle-James eight years ago. It wasn't like she was entitled or anything. Certainly not. But starting off a Monday having to park somewhere else felt wrong to her, jinxed, like it was all downhill from there.

It wasn't all downhill, but it was a close thing.

First thing, the executive assistant she shared with another junior partner handed her a memo from The Hinkle herself. "She wants to see you," Tama whispered. Her wideset brown eyes held a worried glint.

Madison ignored the worry and attempted a friendly smile. "No problem. If you'll rearrange my morning appointments, I'll—"

Tama shook her head. "No can do. IT's here upgrading the servers. All the computers are down."

That would explain the Miata. "Don't you have a paper backup?"

"Sure, but I'll have to dig for the numbers." Tama's bow mouth twisted into a frown. "You ok?"

"Sure," Madison gritted out through the smile she refused to drop. Just because her day was going to the crapper, didn't mean she had to go with it. "How long will the servers be down?"

"Eh. He doesn't know. Could be a couple of days." Tama glanced over her shoulder, then lowered her voice. "Have you met him yet?"

"Met who?"

"The IT guy." Tama waggled her perfectly arched eyebrows. "He's totally hot. I can introduce you—"

Madison cut her off with a slash of one hand. "The Hinkle," she reminded her assistant.

Tama's face fell. "Right. Well, maybe another time. From what I heard, he'll be here for a while."

"Great," Madison muttered. More days started off on the wrong foot. "Buzz The Hinkle and let her know I'm on my way, would you?"

Tama bustled off as Madison sorted through her open case files for the ones most likely to interest, or worse, concern, one of the senior partners. In the back of her mind, she sent a silent wish out to the universe that the IT guy's day was going as badly as hers.

The Miata was gone by the time Madison left work, well after everyone else had gone home. The afternoon's two inches of snowfall had turned to slush, then hardened into ice in the shadows against the building. She picked her way gingerly across the short stretch between the building's entrance and her car, and absolutely, positively refused to ponder what a horrible walk she would've had if the IT guy hadn't taken her parking space.

Hinkle had been in a rare mood all day long. That was enough to keep anyone from being grateful for small favors.

Madison tucked herself into her car, cranked the engine, contemplated ordering a pizza while it warmed, and ended up picking up Chinese on the way home. Her apartment was a refuge, one of the few places she could relax and be herself. No Hinkles to please, no clients to placate. Also no pet or boyfriend to fill the two bedroom space, but who was counting?

She ate warmish beef lo mein standing up in her kitchen, between the island separating it from the living area and the vintage red, six-burner gas stove she'd treated herself to with her last raise.

If she ever had company, she'd be ready to cook up a storm.

The apartment's emptiness echoed around her, so loudly, she finally gave in and switched on her favorite Pandora station, a carefully cultivated selection of classic piano sonatas. She slumped into the leather sofa dominating the living area and checked her watch. Nine thirty, not anywhere near her bedtime.

With a sigh, she retrieved her laptop and checked her email. Most was just junk (Did she really need a t-shirt reading "Lawyers Do It Best"?), but a few demanded responses. She jotted a brief response to her mother (Yes, Mom, I'll be home for Christmas. No, I won't be bringing my non-existent boyfriend.) and ran through the rest just as quickly.

The last was from one of the dating sites she'd signed up for the last time her mother had nagged her about being twenty-eight and unmarried. Madison clicked into it and scanned the profiles arrayed across her laptop's screen.

John, 41, Lawrenceville.

She studied the picture. John had a nice smile and had a full head of hair, but a thirteen-year age difference was a bit too wide of a gap.

Mark, 34, Lawrenceville.

Mark was standing in front of an '80s model Camaro and sported an honest-to-goodness mullet.

She shook her head and read the next profile blurb.

Henry, 31, Lawrenceville.

Hunh. She scrolled the email back up to the first profile and read from the top. Lawrenceville, Lawrenceville, Lawrenceville... What a weird coincidence.

Out of curiosity, she read all eight mini-profiles in the email. All eight men listed Lawrenceville as their home city.

She stared at the email, and finally huffed out a perplexed laugh. The Greater Atlanta Area was a huge sprawl. Lawrenceville was only one city within it, and though it had a sizeable population, how crazy was it to get an email from a dating website in which every single match lived there, when she lived miles away on the outskirts of Marietta?

Pretty crazy, she decided after a minute, then deleted the email and powered down her laptop. Another check of her watch, and she groaned. Ten oh two, still plenty of time before bed.

Oh, well. At least she'd get some reading in. She rechecked the front door, making sure it was locked tight, then flipped off the living room lights and settled into bed with a rousing biography of Mary Shelley, sure to put her right to sleep.

Thursday afternoon just after lunch, Tama poked her head into Madison's office. "Ready for our big date tonight?"

Madison glanced up from the brief she was proofreading and stared blankly at her shared assistant. "What date?"

"You know, speed dating. Me and you and a lot of other desperate singles with five minutes to find Mr. Right?" Tama waggled her eyebrows and affected a leer. "Maybe there'll be some hotties in the bunch this time."

Madison slumped over the brief. The last time they'd tried speed dating, it had been her and Tama and a bunch of desperate singles all right, most of whom had treated the singles meet like the meat market it was. Some uninvited attendee old enough to be Tama's father had pinched her on the butt, right there in front of the event's organizer.

Madison hadn't even gotten that much action.

She shook her head and frowned down at the brief. "I should probably work late tonight."

"Nope," Tama said firmly. "It's me and you against the world, kiddo. Now get your work done so we can go meet the men of our dreams."

Tama whirled away and was gone, leaving Madison alone with her brief and the doubts souring her stomach.

An hour later, she finished proofreading between phone calls and emergency questions from fellow partner wannabes. She shifted toward her computer and tried to log in so she could revise the brief, and was locked out of the law firm's network.

Miata Guy was at it again.

Madison gritted her teeth and paged Tama. As soon as her assistant answered the phone, Madison said, "How long are the computers going to be down now?"

"Er," Tama said. "A couple of hours?"

Madison flipped her wrist over and checked the time. A couple of hours would be after the courts closed. "I have to file this brief by the end of the week, the sooner, the better. Can you check with the IT guy and see if he can do something? I don't know. Route me through another network or something?"

"Sure thing, boss."

Madison hung up and dropped her head into her hands. Ok, the brief had to be filed by Friday at noon. If the Internet didn't come back up, what were her options?

Print it and file a hard copy. Right.

She turned to her computer and was mocked by the log in screen steadfastly holding her work hostage. No computer, no network. No network, no printout. Everything was connected. She couldn't even download a copy of the brief and take it to the FedEx Office for printing.

Tama appeared in her doorway. "Word is the network's down. Fixing it is an all-nighter."

"I hope that's not a metaphor."

"Nope," Tama said in a perky voice. "He's planning on camping out until it's fixed. Said there's a problem with the—"

Madison held up a hand, halting an explanation. "Don't need to know what's wrong, only when I'm going to be able to file this brief."

"First thing in the morning. Now you have no excuse to work late and miss out on our girls' night out."

Tama winked and sashayed away, and Madison slumped into her

chair. Between work and the single scene, she'd much rather have her nose to the grindstone. It figured that IT guy would find a way to muck that up, too.

That evening at seven thirty-five on the dot, Madison followed Tama into a cozy conference room at a posh hotel in downtown Atlanta. Tiny tables had been stationed at regular intervals around the room. Guests mingled at a refreshment table set up against one wall. The décor was tasteful, if minimal, and the lighting was just low enough to hide the worst flaws in anyone's appearance.

Madison twisted her fingers into the handle of her purse. It wasn't too late to back out. A cab wouldn't be that hard to find, and once she got home, she could binge watch *The Big Bang Theory* until bedtime in the safe confines of her apartment.

Tama looped her arm through Madison's. "I know that look."

"What look?"

"The one that says you're about to hightail it out of here."

Madison widened her eyes, affecting innocence. "I have no idea what you're talking about."

"For a lawyer, you're a terrible liar." Tama tugged Madison's arm. "Let's make the rounds and pick out our victims for the night. I'm in the mood for a little Mexican."

"For crying out loud," Madison muttered.

Tama grinned, unrepentant, and away they went, diving feet first into the night's activities.

Madison was assigned a table in the corner. She lined up the pamphlet she'd been given with the table's corner edges, placing it parallel to both with precisely two inches of clearance.

Date number one, a thirty-two-year-old comic book illustrator named Greg, settled down across from her and shot her a friendly smile. He was about her height, athletic under a trendy plaid shirt, and sported a handsome beard the same color as his sleek, black hair.

"Native Southerner or a transplant?" he asked.

"Native," she said promptly, and relaxed under his gentle gaze.

"You?"

"Lawrenceville, born and bred."

The email she'd received from that online dating site popped into her mind. Lawrenceville. What a coincidence.

She cleared her throat and asked, "Ever lived anywhere else?"

"Funny you should mention that," he said. "I just moved back home after living in Boston for four years."

"I've never been."

"You'd love it. The historical sites there are phenomenal, the people are interesting, the food is great. There's just one problem."

She tilted her head to the side, curious in spite of herself. "Yeah?"

He leaned forward and whispered, "They don't sweeten their iced tea until it's already cold. Barbaric, isn't it?"

She laughed and mentally checked *yes* for him. Four minutes later, he shook her hand and moved on, and not long after, date number two sat down at her table.

Where Greg had been lean and polished, Hugh was stocky under the plain black button down he'd tucked into nice jeans. He rubbed a hand over his close-cropped hair and grinned sheepishly at her. "It's my first time."

"My second," she said.

"Yeah? Does it get any easier?"

"Not that I can tell."

He huffed out a laugh and settled more deeply into his chair. "I just got out of the Navy. Six years in the bowels of an aircraft carrier. Not much time for socializing."

"Where were you stationed?"

"San Diego. My mom lives here in Atlanta. She wanted me to spend time near her for a while."

"I don't blame her. Are you from here?"

"Naw, Indiana originally, but my parents moved down here when I was five." He crossed his arms over his wide chest and a slow grin spread across his face. "Know what I missed the most about the South?"

"The perpetual traffic on two eighty-five?"

He laughed. "Naw, the sweet tea. Man, they just don't know how to make it anywhere else."

The back of Madison's neck tingled. She rubbed a hand across her nape, only half her attention on Hugh's rumbling conversation. Two men enjoying sweet tea did not a pattern make. It was just a coincidence, kind of like getting an email full of potential dates, all of whom lived in Lawrenceville.

Three minutes later, she shook hands with Hugh and waited for date number three, Alan from Midtown. He slid into the seat half a minute later sporting a cocksure grin and manicured fingernails.

Madison mentally checked *no*. Any man whose nails were nicer than hers probably had some vanity issues. Still, he was here and deserved a fair shot. She mustered a smile and lobbed the first salvo. "Ice cream or frozen custard?"

"Gelato." He leaned his forearms on the table and threaded his fingers together. "I know this little place outside Rome..."

Madison stifled a yawn and forced her attention on Alan's rambling monologue, which jumped from his last trip to Rome, to his last trip to Athens, to his last trip to Hollywood. She took it from his descriptions of all the rich people he'd met and all the rich things he'd done that he didn't mean the cities of the same names in Georgia.

Pretentious prick.

She firmed her lips against the comment and waited it out. Two out of three wasn't bad, and even if those two turned out to be the only decent guys she met, the night hadn't been a total wash.

The bell rang a boring five minutes after Alan sat down. He stood, his eyes already on the next table. Just as he was turning away, a little devil tapped Madison on her shoulder, prompting her to ask, "How do you feel about unsweetened iced tea?"

He blanched. "Are you kidding? I hate the stuff. Give me Grandma's sweet sun tea any day."

Madison sat back in her chair and pressed her palms flat against the table, her fingers spread wide. Three men who liked sweet tea. No, that wasn't a pattern. It was the South. Everybody liked pre-sweetened iced tea, kind of like everybody conveniently forgot what a turn signal was when driving. Sweet tea was so pervasive in the South, nobody questioned it.

So why was she focusing on it now?

She huffed out a sigh and pasted a smile on her face just as date number four slid into the vacant seat across from her. She refused to mention the tea thing, just refused to.

But she didn't have to. Dates four through ten all mentioned it on their own, all because they'd recently been outside the South and had to endure the unsweetened stuff or drink something else.

Two or three men mentioning a favorite drink wasn't a pattern, but maybe ten was.

She turned in her pamphlet at the end of the event and allowed Tama to lead her through the rest of their evening, while in the back of her mind, she contemplated coincidences and dating and that fickle thing humans call fate.

The next morning, the Miata was parked in her space again, shining like a red beacon under the heavy clouds capping the lot.

Resigned, Madison hunted through the empty spots for one that wouldn't get her coffee spiked with something nasty, and finally found one on the outer edges, as far away from the door as it was possible to get without leaving the parking lot.

Halfway to the door, the angry sky roiling overhead opened up and unleashed a downpour of cold, heavy rain on her unprotected head. She huddled under her briefcase and dashed the remaining distance as fast as her heels could carry her, and ducked under the awning just as lightning popped nearby. Startled, she jerked toward it and nearly plowed headfirst into a man walking out the building's front door.

He grabbed her upper arms, steadying her. "Whoa, there. You ok?"

She glanced down at her soaking wet suit jacket. Thank goodness it was made of a sturdy wool, but her shoes. She tilted one ankle and examined the black leather. Probably ruined.

She shrugged and looked way up into deep green eyes set in a handsome face under nearly black hair. "I'll live. Thanks for catching me."

A slow grin stretched his mouth wide and fine lines crinkled at the corners of his eyes. "Thanks for running into me. It's the best thing that's happened to me all week."

She laughed even as a blush warmed her cheeks. "Sorry about that. Really."

"Don't apologize. You'll ruin the moment."

She shook her head, sending wet curls shimmering around her jawline, and cringed. What a sight she must be, with her hair plastered to her head and her clothes damp with rain, and for crying out loud, she was standing there making a fool of herself with a guy she'd almost run over.

"Gotta go," she muttered, and slipped out of his loose hold and past him.

"Hey, wait," he said, but she was already through the door and into the lobby.

She went straight to the bathroom on her floor, then stared at herself in the mirror, aghast. Mascara pooled beneath her eyes, the foundation she'd applied so carefully had raindrop wide streaks in it, and her hair was the rat's nest she'd imagined it to be. Mortified, she snagged some facial tissue and daubed at the mess her face had become. The first decent man she'd met outside of an arranged meet and look what'd happened.

How could she ever face him again?

She shrugged the thought off and, repairs made, left the bathroom and headed for her office. Chances were good he was a visitor. The building was big, yes, and housed more than just the law firm, but she knew a lot of the people working there by sight, if not by acquaintance.

Him she would've remembered.

The feel of his lean body bumping into hers warmed her. She shut her office door and leaned against it, flustered all over again. How pathetic was it that a chance run in was the closest thing she'd had to a date in months?

Pretty darn pathetic, she decided, and shoved the entire incident out of her mind.

Tama popped in a moment later and grimaced. "Got caught in the rain, huh?"

"No, it just seemed efficient to shower with my clothes on," Madison said evenly. "Did you need something?"

"Network's back up, and you have appointments." Tama glanced down at the spiral bound notebook in her hand. "Three today, the first in an hour. I've already put the folders on your desk. Need me to do anything before then?"

"Can you run home and get me a dry suit?"

Tama went stock still. "Uh, sure?"

Madison sighed. "I was kidding. Just let me know when the first appointment arrives."

"Sure thing, boss."

Madison slipped her jacket off and hung it on the back of her chair. It had taken the brunt of the rain, leaving her shirt relatively dry, but her shoes were sopping wet. She kicked them off under her desk, flicked stray water droplets off her mostly dry skirt, and settled into her chair with the brief she should've filed yesterday.

An hour later when Tama buzzed through the first appointment, Madison was almost dry and the brief had been dealt with. She slipped on her jacket and buttoned it, then stood and faced the doorway, her bare feet hidden behind the bulk of her desk.

Tama opened the door and introduced the tall, dark-headed man behind her as Oliver Knight.

Madison pasted a smile on her face and exchanged pleasantries with Mr. Knight, then sat down and opened the file Tama had prepped for her. "My assistant summarized the reason for your appointment for me, but would you please tell me in your own words why you'd like to hire Hinkle-James?"

He rested a sultry gaze on her as his face dimpled into a smile. "Are you married?"

She blinked once. "I don't discuss my personal life with clients."

"I'm not a client yet, but I'll play along."

He crossed an ankle over a knee and launched into a succinct recounting of a troubled business partnership.

Madison jotted notes on a blank sheet of a legal pad, probed deeper when needed, and otherwise developed a feel for the nature of Mr. Knight's problem. When she had a firm grasp of the situation, she flipped the file closed and folded her hands together on top of it. "You have several options, Mr. Knight—"

"Oliver, please," he said, and his dimples flashed. "I have a feeling we're going to be good friends."

By the way he emphasized *friends*, she doubted very much that friendship was what he had in mind.

She hauled the conversation back on topic and, half an hour later, buzzed Tama to escort Mr. Knight out, satisfied that she'd hooked another client.

Not because he wanted to date her, but because she was just that good.

The next appointment arrived as Mr. Knight was leaving. Madison's heart sank as soon as she spotted the arrival's dark hair and tall, athletic build.

Remy Morrison, an existing client with a penchant for groping any woman stupid enough to landed within easy reach of him.

She sighed, pressed her lips into a firm line. Why hadn't she handed him off to a more experienced attorney?

Her toes brushed against the wet leather of her shoes. Right. Because she needed this job, and in order to keep it, sometimes she had to deal with letches.

Tama was kind enough to sit in on the meeting, notebook held at the ready. Her presence did not one thing to stifle Mr. Morrison's flirtations. At one point, he interrupted Madison's rundown of an upcoming trial to tell her how beautiful she looked, and would she like to continue their conversation over lunch in his hotel room?

Tama bit her lower lip, stifling what Madison was sure would've been a snicker.

Both of them managed to evade Mr. Morrison's roaming hands, but by the time appointment number three rolled around, exhaustion had gnawed a huge chunk out of Madison's patience.

Tama opened the door and introduced yet another tall, dark, and handsome man, this one named Todd Hennessy. Mr. Hennessy had the grace to temper his flirtations with good sense. Only once did he suggest anything untoward, and that was a simple request to meet him for drinks later.

She demurred, ignored the disappointment replacing his dimpled smile, and as soon as he left, Madison buzzed Tama to let her know she was calling it quits for the day. One tall, dark, and handsome man had been enough for her, and she'd met him first thing. Maybe if she'd stopped there, her day would've ended on a high note.

That evening after pizza and four episodes of *The Big Bang Theory*, Madison readied for bed in a much better mood than when she'd come home. Amazing what an evening spent doing exactly what one wanted could do for a body, especially with not a single letch in sight.

After brushing her teeth, she pulled out the laptop she'd ignored the entire evening and checked her email. Half a dozen dating site messages awaited her, right below an email from her mom.

Madison plopped onto the edge of her bed, set the laptop down beside her, and frowned at it as trepidation filled her. True, she hadn't checked her messages in a couple of days, but she hadn't been active on the site either. She didn't usually get that many messages unless she actively browsed matches, and she hadn't had time to do that in the past couple of days.

Curiosity prodded her to check her inbox on the dating site. She logged into her account and studied the tag lines next to thumbnails of each man. Different hair colors and styles, different expressions, different localities, different...

She scrolled up and down the screen again and sighed. Every man was thirty-two years old.

For crying out loud, how many coincidences did one woman have to suffer through in such a short period of time?

She logged out of the dating site, jotted a quick note to her mom (No, Mom, I'm not bringing Mr. Right to Dad's birthday party, but I will as soon as I find him.), and climbed into bed with a trashy romance, in which at least two people were guaranteed a happy ending without a single coincidence ruining the story.

That night, dozens of men appeared in her dreams, each hazy and indistinct except for their smile: familiar, warm, flirtatious, knowing. Madison shifted restlessly under the covers as her subconscious mind struggled to place it. She knew that smile, knew it from somewhere, but where?

The dreams shifted from place to place, flashing by focal points. Her sofa, positioned precisely atop the antique rug she'd scrimped for months to buy. Her desk, the only barrier between her and her clients. A red Miata, bright under the winter sun.

A dimpled smile.

She woke on a gasp and her eyes popped open. Light bled through the curtained windows, too dim for sunrise. *Brian,* the dream whispered, and she rubbed it away, her hands shaky on her sweat coated skin.

What was it with men lately?

Or was the universe playing tricks on her?

Madison rolled over in bed, punched her pillow into shape, and flopped into it. The odd coincidences she'd experienced recently flashed through her mind one by one. She fell asleep ticking them off in her mind, going over and over them searching for some hint of meaning, and eventually fell into a fitful sleep.

She woke the next morning with a clear purpose, spurred as much by need as confusion. Another perspective would help, and not just any perspective. She needed another single woman to hash it all out with, preferably someone with a wide-open mind and a wacky way of viewing life.

And she knew exactly who that person should be.

Madison rushed through her morning routine, took a bare moment to make sure her skirt matched her jacket, and her shoes matched both, then dashed out the apartment door toward her car. The sun was bright in the early morning sky amid pink and gold clouds, and the city flared to life around her as she drove.

The Miata was parked in her space again. She passed right by it without a second thought and parked in a brand-new associate's space.

You snooze, you lose.

Madison hurried inside and into the elevator, fidgeted the entire way up, and scurried out of it straight toward her assistant's desk through the nearly empty office. She met Tama halfway there as Tama walked out of the copy room, and crooked a finger at her.

"In my office now, please," Madison said, and hooked her arm through Tama's to make sure she didn't get lost on the way.

"Whoa there, boss," Tama said, but Madison just picked up the pace and hurried them toward her office, their heels muted thuds against the industrial carpeting.

As soon as they were both inside, Madison shut the door and locked it, then veered around Tama and dropped into the chair behind her desk.

Tama stood exactly where Madison had planted her, her bow mouth pulled into a frown. "What in the world?"

A sigh shuddered out of Madison. She yanked off her winter coat, then ran a calming hand over her the messy bun she'd twisted her hair into. "I need to talk to you."

"Ok," Tama said, drawing the word out.

"I mean, I need to talk to somebody and you're just crazy enough to understand."

"That had to sound better in your head." Tama dropped the files she held onto Madison's desk and perched on the edge of one of the visitor's chairs. "The doctor is in the house. Spill it."

So Madison did, starting with the email she'd received from the dating site. "Eight men, all living in Lawrenceville," she said, then tacked on the tidbits about the speed dates. "They'd all travelled out of town recently, and every single one mentioned how good sweet tea was in the South. Can you believe it?"

"Sweet tea in the South," Tama murmured. "Happy thought."

Madison held her hands up, palms out. "I know it sounds crazy."

"It sounds something, all right. I'm guessing there's more."

There was, and it all tumbled out of Madison in a flurry of words, how she'd met four men in one day who were the same height and build, who had the same hair color and smiles and flirty nature, then the messages from half a dozen men, all aged thirty-two, and the kicker, the dreams she'd had, so indistinct, the only things she could remember were a lot of men and a single name.

"Brian," she said, then slumped back into her chair and stared at Tama's smug smile, miserable to the core. "Now that I've said it, it doesn't seem like that big a deal, but when I was living it? Wow. I mean, wouldn't you have freaked out with all those coincidences piling up?"

Tama leaned forward and crossed her arms together on top of the desk. "Brian, huh?"

Madison threw her hands up in the air and let them fall limply into her lap. "That's what you got out of all that ranting?"

"It's the most important thing."

"Maybe to you," Madison muttered. "But what does it mean? I mean, it has to mean something doesn't it, or am I making a mountain out of random events?"

Tama stood abruptly. "Oh, I think there's definitely a mountain here. You were bound to find out sooner or later."

"Find out what?"

"No, no. Let me surprise you. I'll be back in a jiff."

"Back?" Madison said, but Tama whirled away and out the door without responding.

Madison clenched her hands into fists against her thighs, the events of the past few days a continual loop in her mind. Yeah, it sounded crazy, now that she'd said it out loud. Tama was probably going to call the psych ward, or worse, she was on her way to tell The Hinkle that Madison had finally gone around the bend. One too many briefs, probably. Either that or all the letches.

A soft knock hit the door, then it opened on Tama. Behind her stood the guy Madison had almost mowed down the day before.

Madison scrambled into a stand and gawped. "You."

The man stuck his hands in the pockets of his khakis and grinned sheepishly. "Yeah. I kinda hoped we'd run into each other again."

Tama cut her eyes at him, one corner of her mouth tilted upward. "Oh, you were going to run into her tomorrow. She's next on your list."

"What list?" Madison asked.

"*Brian* is our IT guy," Tama said.

Madison's mouth formed a silent *oh*. So that's who'd been hijacking her parking spot.

"He's thirty-two," Tama continued, "lives in Lawrenceville, loves sweet tea, and just got back from a trip to Hong Kong."

Brian glanced at Tama, his black eyebrows arched high. "Shouldn't I be the one telling her that?"

"Yes," Tama said, her perky voice emphatic. "I'll just leave you two alone for a good chat."

She pivoted around and walked to the door, then turned and mouthed to Madison, "He's a keeper."

Brian held his hand out to Madison. "Nice to officially meet you."

"Yeah, it is." Laughter bubbled up, ending in a sloppy grin Madison tried hard to restrain, and failed. "Sorry. You wouldn't believe the week I'm having."

Brian cupped her hand in both his and squeezed, warming her from head to toe. "Why don't you tell me about it over dinner tonight? I know this great Mom and Pop. The sweet tea there is out of this world."

A laugh spilled out in spite of her best efforts. "I bet," she said.

And it was.

A MUTUAL FEELING

They came for Alice on a Wednesday morning.

She hurried to the door with her chopping knife in her hand, seven inches of muted steel, another six devoted to the carved, wooden hilt. It was a good knife, perfectly balanced, razor sharp edge. A Christmas present from her husband John, who hadn't bothered to lever himself out of his recliner and answer the door. She'd had to come all the way from the kitchen, leaving the celery for Thanksgiving's stuffing wilting on her kitchen counter.

And now, last minute shoppers crowded the stores and she had no time to get fresh, what with company coming and twenty people to feed tomorrow evening, and pies and cakes still to be made.

She swung the door open, knife in hand, and stared at the half dozen men dressed in SWAT gear pointing wickedly intricate guns at her from the other side.

"Put your weapon down," the lead man barked. "Put down the fucking knife!"

She glanced at it, puzzled. A strand of celery fiber clung to the edge, distorting her blurry reflection. It was just a knife. A big knife, yes, but just a knife. What was the big deal? She lifted it toward the lead man, a peace offering. His gun popped and reared back against his shoulder, and a burning zing cut through Alice's chest. She fell down, down, down, only dimly aware of men swarming past her into the house and icy blue eyes staring dispassionately at her beneath a hard, black helmet.

They came for Alice on a Saturday afternoon.

She poked her head into the living room, chopping knife in hand. Dadgum sales people. Couldn't they leave a body in peace to fix supper and have a nice, relaxing evening at home? And there was John, slouched into his recliner, two empty beer bottles dripping condensation onto the coffee table.

She reined in her impatience, blew it out on a long exhale. "John, honey, would you get the door?"

"Game," he grunted, and she rolled her eyes as she scurried through the house and opened the damn thing herself.

Half a dozen men dressed in SWAT uniforms stood on the other side, aiming an array of black, metal-barreled guns at her.

"Um, hello," she said.

"Alice Humboldt?" the lead man asked.

"I'm Alice, yes."

"Drop your weapon and raise your hands above your head."

Bob from next door shambled to the end of his driveway, only his bobbing, black head visible over the men scattered along her front porch. He checked his mail, glanced up, grinned his toothsome car salesman smile. "That's some company you've got there, Alice. Card game later?"

"Sure, Bob. Tell Lou I'll bring the chips."

Alice raised her hand in a half-hearted wave. The knife glinted in the sunlight, throwing a reflection into the lead man's icy blue eyes. *Pop, pop.* His gun recoiled sharply into his shoulder. Something burst inside her, something vital and warm and liquid, and down she went in a barrage of harsh male orders and eyes as cold as an Arctic wind.

* * *

Alice woke screaming, clutching the burning agony ripping through her chest, trapped in an echo of gunfire and barked epithets. Hurt, God, it hurt so much. The blood. Her knife. John on the recliner.

She gasped and sat bolt upright. The baby!

Covers flipped back, exposing her bare legs to the night cooled air. Scurrying down the hallway, peeking into the baby's room, and a relieved sigh. There the baby was, curled up against her teddy, thumb in her mouth, sleeping peacefully as babies should. Alice tucked the covers over her sweetie's shoulders, ran a hand along the soft, downy hair. She clucked her tongue softly. Still not grown out, and the baby nearly a year old now.

A year, already.

With a final sigh, Alice crept out of the baby's room and down the stairs, her anxiety lessening with each step. John was still in his recliner in front of a football game replaying on the TV, right where she'd left him when she'd climbed up the stairs and crawled into bed.

This was real, her family, her home, not the nightmare she'd awakened to. Not blood and pain and dark claws dragging her into death.

She rubbed a hand over the throb lingering in her chest. Just a nightmare, she thought, and put it out of her mind. Breakfast didn't fix itself, and it sure didn't keep the house clean or the laundry done.

Later, after breakfast and lunch were made and eaten, after the floors were mopped and the car washed and a nice, thick stew started for supper, a knock banged on the door, loud and insistent.

Alice's heart pattered a rapid beat in her throat and her hands paused in the middle of chopping cabbage. She stared at the knife, its sharp edge gleaming in the overhead light John had installed on her last birthday. A present for his beloved wife, just like the knife and the thick-bottomed, ceramic coated pot cooking supper's stew.

He was a good husband, he was. Thoughtful, even.

But the knife.

Bile churned in her gut around a cold dread. She carefully set the knife on the counter beside the chopping board, straightened the cranberry colored sweater she wore. The knock came again, accompanied by the rough slap of her name.

She walked out of the kitchen into the living room past John in his recliner and the beer bottles he refused to recycle, each step a slog through viscous molasses. The door loomed in front of her, a deep red rectangle, plain on this side, adorned with a Christmas wreath on the other.

To greet company, like Bob and Lou and the family coming in to celebrate the holidays.

But it wasn't Bob on the other side of the door. For some reason, cool, blue eyes popped into Alice's mind. Her hand trembled as she turned the knob and opened the door, and there they were, those eyes from her nightmare. Unfeeling, glacial, lacking depth or feeling or the tiniest shred of humanity.

She flicked her gaze over the half dozen men standing on her porch, all bristling with weapons she couldn't name, then turned it on the lead man. Icy eyes, a face set in granite beneath a hard, black helmet.

"I'm Alice," she said softly. "I'm... I'm Alice."

"Drop the weapon," he barked. "Hands where I can see them."

She shook her head, so confused. She'd left the knife in the kitchen. John didn't even own a gun. The baby. Alice had insisted when she'd gotten pregnant, hadn't she? But the memory was dim, a bare sketch in her head, drowned out by the fear pounding through her blood behind every galloping heartbeat.

"I'm not armed," she said, her voice scarcely a whisper. "I don't have a weapon."

A man standing at the bottom of the stairs spat onto the sidewalk. A jagged scar bisected his right cheek and his hands were steady on his gun. "Just shoot her. We don't got all day."

"No," the lead man said. "The regs state—"

The scarred man lifted his rifle, aimed, and pulled the trigger in a practiced ballet. The bullet slammed into Alice's shoulder, spinning her around as the lead man's mouth twisted into a curse and John's football game droned on and on in the background.

The days blurred together, a stygian film clinging to Alice's existence, slimy and surreal.

At first, only the nightmares she endured each night tied the days together. The cold-eyed man didn't knock on her door every day or in any pattern she could discern, but when he did, it always ended in death, always.

And she began to remember, began to mark the days on her calendar, and when that didn't work, when her tidy little exes disappeared overnight and the pages of the Farm and Garden annual calendar refused to budge away from the wall, she gouged them into the chopping board with the tip of her knife.

Those stayed. Those she could count on.

Twenty-three days passed, by her count, and of those, the cold-eyed man came seventeen times. Seventeen visits, seventeen bullets in her chest, each miraculously gone when she next awoke. Not even one scar remained, but the nightmares, they shook her.

She stopped trying to communicate with John.

Alice bore down on the knife, venting her anger in rough slices of thick carrots. What was the point? He'd been like this the entire length of their marriage, always sitting in his damn recliner, always ignoring her in favor of some sports program. So many years, so goddamn many years...

She frowned and carefully prodded her mind for a date, a memory, anything to tie her to the man occupying the living room, anything beyond the irritation of his cloying presence. Those blasted beer bottles, dripping moisture onto the coffee table, the hand-carved, one-of-a-kind wooden table he'd gifted her with when the baby was born.

The gifts were there, every single one, every event they were supposed to commemorate, but there was nothing else. Just...nothing.

The knife slipped and, in her fumbling haste to catch a shower of carrot slices, the tip slashed across her finger. Bright red blood welled through the cut, threatening to slide off her skin into the evening meal.

Alice cursed under her breath and rushed to the sink, cupping the wounded digit in her free hand. What was wrong with her lately? This obsession with the past was unhealthy, a blight on her otherwise perfect existence.

Well, near perfect, anyway. So what if John was a grunting, hirsute lump in the living room? So what if they hadn't talked in ages, really talked, not the *hey, I'm busies* that passed for conversation lately? So what if they hadn't had sex in so long, the sensation of sensual pleasure was lost to her? Lots of married people lived like that and were perfectly happy.

She flipped on the faucet and stuck her finger under crystal clear water. Bob and Lou were happy, weren't they? And they'd been married...

Alice frowned at the pink tinged water flowing down the drain. For the life of her, she couldn't remember how long Bob and Lou had been married, but it had to be two decades at least.

And they'd endured. They'd survived, a happily married couple holding on through thick and thin, through sickness and health and sorrow and memory loss.

The cut sealed together under the balm of frigid fluid. Alice shut the tap off and snagged a paper towel, wrapped it gingerly around the now-healed wound. Careless, that's what all this thinking did to her. She'd have to be more careful. There was the baby to think of, after all, and God above knew John wouldn't lift a finger to care for the infant if something happened to Alice.

She was ready the next time they came, ready to do anything if it kept the bullet in the gun and her baby safe and sound. She was in the kitchen, knife in hand when they knocked. Wasn't she always in the kitchen slicing her way through a never-ending supply of vegetables?

But the weather was different. A slushy snow had fallen overnight, covering the neighborhood's tidy lawns beneath half a foot of pristine white. Innocence. Peace. Beauty. A lovely way to begin any day.

Alice set her knife on the counter, marveled at her own lack of nerves, and stepped carefully around the island out of the kitchen into the living room, ignoring John's muttered grunts and the empty beer bottle crushing the early Valentine's Day card she'd given him. The door rattled under a heavy fist. Her heart leapt once, then settled into a steady rhythm. Calm propriety. That's what she'd try this time, and if that didn't work, she could always try begging.

Again.

She wrapped her hand around the doorknob, turned it with one swift twist, and swung it open on the same icy blue eyes, the same hawkish nose, the same soft lips. They were an anomaly, those lips were. The upper one was flat and straight, but the lower one was a generous curve. Dimple lines bracketed his mouth, hinting at laughter and warmth, characteristics otherwise lacking amid the harsh, brutally rugged crags of his face.

Too bad this man's personality wasn't more like his lips and less like his eyes.

She pasted a friendly smile on her own face and focused on his mouth. "Hello. Can I help you?"

"Alice Humboldt?" the man barked.

"Why, yes, that's me."

"Drop your weapon and raise your hands."

Alice held her hands out, palms up, the only gesture she'd ever made that hadn't gotten her killed outright. "Would you like a mug of hot cocoa? I can make some fresh for you."

"I said drop your weapon and raise your hands!"

"I don't have a weapon," she replied, forcing her words out in stiff politeness even as her heart tripped and thudded in her chest. "It's far too cold out to linger on the porch. Won't you come in for some cocoa?"

The tip of the man's gun wavered and a small vee appeared between thick, black eyebrows. "Lady, I don't know what game you're playing—"

"Oh, I'm not," she assured him.

"—but I'm not interested in your fucking cocoa. I'm interested in detaining a suspected terrorist—"

Alice burst out laughing. "A terrorist, here? This is Suburbia."

The man with the scarred face spat into the snow, then twisted his mouth into a grotesque smile. "That's where they grow 'em best, right Will?"

The man in front of Alice narrowed his eyes at her. "Yes, sir. Terrorists hide in plain sight out here, waiting to be activated. Likely keep all their bomb-making supplies in the garage."

"A Volvo," Alice said faintly. "That's all I have in my garage. Your name is Will?"

He muttered a curse under his breath and leveled the gun's barrel at her. "We've wasted enough time. Put your goddamn hands up so we can get on with it."

"Get on with what?" she asked, and clamped her mouth shut around a mingled mixture of fear and exasperation. Knowing why these men kept showing up on her door would go a long way toward helping her deal with them, wouldn't it? On the other hand, all she really wanted was for them to go away and leave her and her family alone.

Will's brows shot down and he opened his mouth. The baby screamed from her room on the second floor. Alice whirled toward the stairs, unthinking, automatically shifting from soon-to-be victim to mother. Out of the corner of her eye, a black barrel glinted in the sun, stark against the snow covered ground, and a report rang through the neighborhood.

But it wasn't Will, not this time. The thought struck her hard as the bullet ripped through her shoulder, propelling her into the gleaming wooden newel at the bottom of the staircase. Will cursed long and low, and gentle hands caught her, lowering her to the hardwood floor among a cacophony of booted feet thudding through her home and a baby crying for her mother.

A steady, mechanical blip woke Alice three seconds before pain flooded into her, a raging tide of hot agony throbbing in time to the blip's rhythm, slightly offbeat. *Blip*-throb, *blip*-throb, *blip*-throb. She winced and reached for her shoulder, and was drawn up short by something firm wrapped around her wrist, holding it down by her side.

Her eyes flew open and her gaze filled with the oddest sight. She was lying flat on her back, strapped to a hospital bed in a stark white, sterile room. A man sat in a chair beside her, head down, forearms on thighs, hands dangling between his widespread knees. His hair was gleaming black and rumpled, his shoulders broad under a thin, clingy t-shirt.

Even from this angle she recognized Will, the man who'd killed her time and again for as far back as she could remember. Not John or her father or any number of men she knew, but Will, a trained killer and a near stranger.

He glanced up and fixed those pale blue eyes on her. "You're awake."

She pressed her lips together, containing laughter or hysteria or panic, which she wasn't sure. "Yes," she said as solemnly as she could. "I'm awake. Where's John? My husband?"

"Watching the baby."

Will's voice was flat and nearly as cold as his eyes, and she had the sudden, awful feeling there was something he wasn't telling her.

She cleared her throat, jangled the leather manacle chaining her to the hospital bed. "Is this really necessary?"

Tanned cheeks flushed pink, and Will's gaze dropped to his hands. "Procedure."

"Because I'm a terrorist?"

"Suspected." He sighed, a short gust of air, and sat straight up. "Look, lady—"

"Alice," she said softly. "My name is Alice Humboldt."

"Alice," he repeated, and oddly, his own voice softened. "We got a tip about you. Had to follow up on it, yeah?"

"Of course."

"It was supposed to be a quick in-and-out. Identify, verify, and eliminate."

"Eliminate," she said flatly.

His eyelashes fluttered so slightly she would've missed it if she hadn't been studying him. "I'm just doing my job."

"By *eliminating* a housewife and mother?" She rolled her head on the pillow and shifted her gaze from him to the plain white ceiling. "Why are you doing this? I've never even had a speeding ticket."

"Maybe if you hadn't answered the door carrying a weapon—"

She did laugh then. The harsh retort echoed against the empty walls, filling the dead silence between the constant beep of the machine blipping her vitals. "I left my chopping knife in the kitchen."

His eyes lost the small measure of warmth his blush had carried into them. "Fucking knife was in your hand when I caught you."

"I left it in the kitchen," she gritted out. "Because you keep killing me. You keep accusing me of being something I'm not. You keep—"

"Doing my job?" He raked a hand through his hair, broad palm, elegant fingers, and scrubbed the back of his neck. "Look, lady, I don't know what you're babbling on about—"

"Babbling!"

"—but I wasn't the one gunning for you. Regs state—"

"I don't give a flip about regulations."

"—that an enemy combatant—"

"Enemy combatant!" she screeched, and jerked her wrists against the manacles encircling them. "Where in the world did you get that idea?"

He paused in mid-sentence, closed his mouth, and slumped against the chair's metal back. "I don't know. You were just one in a series of raids we were supposed to make today."

"And yet here we are." She thumped the back of her head into the pillow and resumed staring at the ceiling. Boring it might be, but at least it wasn't trying to kill her. "I want John."

Will coughed into a balled up fist. "Ah, about that."

Oh, she knew that tone. It was the same one she'd been reduced to over the past few weeks while trying to deal with an unresponsive husband. "Let me guess. He wouldn't get out of his recliner."

"Ma'am, I couldn't even get him to look at me."

"The baby?"

"I, ah." Will coughed again, resettled his booted feet against the brilliantly polished white floor. "I brought the basinet downstairs and set it and the baby beside him."

"Thank you." It was all she could say, given the circumstances. He could've just left the baby upstairs or called Social Services. How many other men would've made the time to take care of the small child of a suspected terrorist? "Next time—"

"Next time? Are you fucking nuts?" He slapped his hands on his thighs and stood, towering over her next to the bed, his cold eyes boring into her. "I'm straightening this out today, Mrs. Humboldt, so there won't be a next time."

He nodded sharply and strode off, and disappeared into the fog comprising the far edges of the room beyond a lone computer station near the end of her bed. Her gaze drifted to it once he was gone, drifted and fixed as her mind twisted around trying to make some sort of sense out of her conversation with Will.

She was a suspected terrorist, an enemy combatant, for crying out loud. No wonder Will's team kept trying to kill her. No wonder they kept coming after her.

And in spite of what he'd said, she knew, as surely as she knew her name, that there would be a next time no matter what straightening Will tried to do on her behalf.

Alice woke alone in her bed surrounded by the calming scents of lavender and cinnamon. She lifted one hand, jangled it, and exhaled a relieved sigh. Home and free, exactly where she should be. No more manacles, no more hospitals filled with a lifeless fog. Just her and the baby and John in the home they'd built together.

She stuffed her bare feet into slippers, shrugged her robe on, and tromped down the stairs, yawning as her mind turned over the vast array of chores needing her attention. Breakfast first, then laundry and bathrooms. She risked peeking out the living room window, grunted at the frost covered ground, and wound her way between the mercifully clean coffee table and John sitting in front of a blackened TV screen. Washing the car could wait a while. Maybe she'd drive into town later and run it through the car wash.

The kitchen light was already on when Alice stepped through the open doorway. The island counter sparkled in the brightness, festooned with her favorite wooden chopping block and her knife. She yawned and stretched as she ambled to the fridge, fumbled for the handle and opened it, then stared at the empty shelves.

Where were the vegetables? She bent down, yanked open the crisper, and snapped her mouth shut. Where were the milk and the eggs and the deli meat for today's lunch?

Befuddled, she closed the fridge door and opened the freezer, and was greeted by a blast of ice cold air and a bare vault. No ice, no home-frozen baggies of vegetables neatly labeled with date and contents, no turkey bought at Thanksgiving and saved for Easter's feast.

Alice shut the freezer door and slouched against the fridge, shocked to her core. Where had all their food gone? Had someone snuck in during the night and stolen it?

She shook her head, denying the conjecture as soon as it entered her mind. No one would waltz into her house, empty out the contents of the refrigerator, and leave the TV untouched.

But if not that, then what?

Maybe she was going crazy. Maybe her brief stint in the hospital had pushed her over the edge and she was imagining it. She laughed, a short, humorless bark of hard air and raw disbelief. Maybe that first time Will had shot her, she'd really died and was now living in a surreal, suburban hell.

She checked the fridge again, just to be sure, found both it and the freezer empty, and shrugged. Nope, not her imagination. Nothing for it, then. John might be immune to hunger, but she and the baby weren't. A trip to the grocery store wouldn't eat into the day too much. If worse came to worse, she could always clean the bathrooms tomorrow. It wasn't like they were going anywhere.

After a quick shower, she pulled on fresh jeans and a cranberry colored sweater, checked on the baby sleeping soundly in her crib, and hopped down the stairs. "Going to town," she told John, and didn't bother responding to his hoarse grunt.

She snagged her purse, placed a hand on the doorknob. Three loud booms sounded against the door, and an all-too-familiar voice called, "Police! Open up!"

And that was the straw that broke her. For weeks now, she'd lived under the threat of these hooligans showing up, shooting her for no reason at all that she could find, terrorizing her while she was trying to deal with a failing marriage, a soon-to-be toddler, and an empty fridge. There was only so much a woman could take, and that was it for her.

She yanked open the door and zeroed in on Will, steady as a rock Will with his broad, muscled shoulders and arctic eyes and sweetly kissable mouth. "Here to kill me again, Will?"

The tip of Will's gun wavered and he blinked, just once. "Ma'am?"

"Don't you ma'am me, you blue-eyed, cold-blooded ruffian." She stabbed a finger at him and waggled it for good measure. "I have had it up to here with you and your gun-bedecked goon squad. No more. Do you hear me, Will? No more."

The scarred-face man lowered his gun and frowned at her. "I think something's wrong."

She whirled on him, so mad she could spit. "You bet your darn toodles, there's something wrong. How many times do you have to show up on my door and kill me before you figure out I'm not a dadgum terrorist?"

Will lowered his gun and held out a placating hand. "Now listen, lady. We're just—"

"Doing your job?" she retorted.

Will's expression, so impersonal before, hardened into granite. "Something wrong with keeping people safe?"

Alice's anger evaporated as abruptly as it had formed, leaving her empty and weary and a little embarrassed at her own temerity. Alice Humboldt, mild-mannered housewife and mother of one, did not confront the police in public, and especially not on her own front porch in the middle of winter with heated air leaching out the gaping entrance.

She stepped onto the porch, shut the door behind herself, and ignored the blush staining her cheeks. "I have to go to the grocery store. Maybe you could shoot me after I get back."

Will's mouth twisted into a grimace. "We're not here to shoot you, lady."

"My name is Alice Humboldt," she said, enunciating every syllable. "You should remember it after all this time."

She swept past him and the four men still aiming their weapons at her, bounced down the stairs onto the walkway past the scarred man and his scowl. The garage door was already open. The Volvo was waiting for her, exactly where it should be, and humor transformed her embarrassment into a grin. No thieves after all, though that didn't explain the lack of fresh vegetables in her fridge. Odd that they'd disappeared when she'd never been without before.

She paused with her hand on the Volvo's driver's side door and frowned. Odd that she'd never before considered where the vegetables came from, wasn't it? And odder still, she couldn't recall actually shopping before that moment. Oh, she knew she had. How else could food have appeared in her house? But she couldn't remember the details of any single shopping trip, couldn't even, after a ruthless bout of prodding, remember where the grocery store was.

"Need some help?"

Alice shrieked and whirled on the man towering over her, and looked up into cold blue eyes. "Goodness, Will. Don't sneak up on a body like that."

He shrugged one shoulder, jostling the gun held in his hands. "Jack sent me 'round to make sure you weren't going to blow us up while he checked in with HQ."

"Blow you...?" She stifled a thready laugh and swept a hand around the cavernous garage, bare of tools, clutter, and grime. "With what?"

"Your car."

"My car," she repeated, and shook her head, baffled by him and the entire situation. "It's a Volvo. I'm pretty sure they don't blow up unless you're really trying."

He grunted. "It could happen."

"Only in your imagination," she said sweetly, and had the pleasure of watching him blink again. Good. She was tired of being the only befuddled human in her life. She lifted the door handle and said, "Can I go now? I want to get back before the baby wakes."

Will cupped a hand over hers resting on the Volvo, stopping her. "I don't get it."

"Get what?"

"You don't feel like a terrorist."

"Probably because I'm not," she said, then couldn't help herself or her blasted curiosity. "What exactly does a terrorist feel like?"

"Not a PYT."

"A PYT?" She shook her head, yet again lost. "I don't speak cop."

He grinned and eased away from her, dropping his gloved hand off hers. "Maybe you should learn to speak man."

The radio on his shoulder crackled, then the scarred man's voice said, "All clear. Rendezvous at Checkpoint Gamma."

Will reached up and squeezed the radio, his clear blue eyes steady on her. "Roger that."

"Now can I go?" Alice asked.

"Yes, ma'am." He grinned again and touched a single finger to the rim of his helmet. "You have a good day, Mrs. Humboldt."

He pivoted and strode away, and Alice stared after him, watching until he vanished around the edge of the garage. What a confusing man this Will character was. If she didn't know better, she'd swear he'd just flirted with her, and that after shooting her more than a dozen times.

Learn to speak man, indeed. What sane woman in her right man could even begin to fathom the ins and outs of the masculine sex, let alone speak their language?

She got in the Volvo and put him out of her mind, focusing all her attention on remembering where the grocery store was and not on the warmth of Will's flirtatious smile.

Two weeks passed by Alice's reckoning, fourteen days empty of SWAT and threats and Will. John had gone crazy, she was certain. He never budged from in front of the TV, though it had gone dark and stayed that way no matter what she tried.

She'd finally broken down and picked up the phone to call a repairman, and gotten an endless drone instead of a dial tone.

All around her, things were breaking, and there was nothing she could do about it. The Volvo sputtered out on her second attempt to find a grocery store, but that was ok. Food had appeared in the fridge and cupboards again. Not always the food she wanted to cook, as it had been before, but food nonetheless.

What worried her most was the baby, that sweet, innocent child Alice had birthed a year ago. The baby refused to stand, didn't cry or roll over or do any of the things a child of that age should do. Alice had gotten so frantic, she'd bundled the baby up and taken her next door to Bob and Lou's. Nobody was home, so she'd gone to the next neighbor and the next, and found every house empty.

She'd even tried walking into the fog surrounding the neighborhood. One step in, she'd rebounded off a hard wall and nearly landed on her tush, bobbling the baby in the process.

Still, the baby hadn't cried.

Alice brought the bassinet downstairs and kept it in the kitchen.

Between chopping vegetables and building dishes on the stove, she tried the phone again and again, at a loss as to what else she should be doing. Somebody had to be out there. Somewhere, there had to be somebody who could help.

On the fifteenth day, a hard fist banged into the door. Relief sapped all the strength out of Alice's legs and she sagged against the kitchen island. *Will.* He'd come back, just when she needed help the most. Oh, sure, he kept trying to kill her, but he was with the police and he'd shown compassion for the baby, and Alice knew, deep down where her harshest fears mingled among her greatest hopes, that she could trust him to find help.

She ran through the house past the bassinet and a clean coffee table and a statue-like husband, and yanked open the door. "Will. Thank God you're here."

Will blinked and lowered his gun. "Ma'am?"

The scar-faced man, Jack, spat on the ground and nudged the man standing beside him. "See what I mean?"

The man, a gangly brunette wearing grimy Chucks with his SWAT uniform, grunted. "Yeah, man. That's way off program."

Alice glanced at Will, who looked just as puzzled as she did. "What's off program?" she asked him, her voice low.

He shrugged one shoulder. "Beats me. I thought we were here looking for a terrorist."

"Suspected," she corrected absent-mindedly. "Just once, I'd like you to remember who I am."

"Ma'am?"

She waved his curiosity off and focused on the new man. "Who are you?"

"Developer," he grunted. He glanced down at a small tablet balanced on one palm, frowned, then tapped a rapid sequence across the screen. "How's that?"

Alice shook her head, completely lost. "How's what?"

"Never mind."

He tapped again, and this time, a sharp pain stabbed into Alice's left temple. She hissed in a short breath against the blinding agony and doubled over. The man tapped again, each keystroke a nail in her skull, and she lost her balance and stumbled into the doorframe.

Will slung his gun over his shoulder and caught her, steadying her with one large, broad hand on her arm. "You ok, Alice?"

She glanced up, way up into ice blue eyes, somehow warm and alive. "You remembered."

His mouth twitched into a gentle smile. "I never forget a PYT."

"Why didn't you say anything?"

"You're still a suspected terrorist." His grin widened and a gleam entered his eyes. "And you're still married."

Jack snorted. "That's a new one."

The developer raised his head, did a double take. "He's not supposed to do that."

"No shit, Sherlock," Jack said.

Will glanced around, his expression mild, and just as easily dismissed the lunatic fringe. "How's the Volvo? Turned it into a bomb yet?"

She laughed, winced at the pain still lingering in her head. "Can't even get it to run."

"Shame."

"Oh, for fuck's sake," Jack muttered, and elbowed the developer again. "Do something."

"I'm trying. Jesus, man, it's not easy to track down a rogue game element and reprogram it on the fly." The developer squinted at his laptop's screen, tapped half a dozen more keys, then grinned. "Gotcha."

Screaming agony rolled into Alice, a molten wave unlike anything she'd ever felt, wiping away her humor and frustration, and dimming her vision into a single pinprick of light. Will muttered a curse and yanked her forward against a hard, armor-covered chest, and she stumbled and fell into him, the way a spaceship tumbles headlong into a black hole, and the world righted itself again.

Will, this frost-eyed stranger who kept trying to kill her, steadied her somehow and lent his strength to her just when she needed it most.

Alice's vision blossomed into full view. She turned her head and rested her cheek against nylon-covered Kevlar, and studied the tableau assembled across her front porch. Four other SWAT team members stood rock still, the lethal ends of their rifles pointed straight at her. Jack frowned, twisting his scar into a snake along his cheek. And the developer muttered under his breath and shook his head, intent on the tiny computer held in his hand.

"That should've worked," he said. "I don't get it. I've tried nearly everything and she still..."

Alice narrowed her eyes at him. Yes, in spite of whatever the developer was doing, in spite of being shot and terrorized by these men and increasingly ignored by her once-beloved husband, she was *still*. Still here, still confused, still a housewife and mother. Still, in spite of everything, she was alive.

The realization tingled along her nerves, spreading a new emotion in its wake, something unlike anything she'd ever felt. It took her a moment to recognize it, to measure its fullness and make it a part of herself, but when she did, when fury exploded inside of her, filling her to the brim, it focused laser sharp on the developer.

This man had tried to kill her, not the way Will and Jack and the other SWAT had so that she was reborn again and again into the only life she'd ever known, but end her, permanently. The certainty seeped into her bones the way rain replenishes the earth. The developer had come to Suburbia to wipe Alice off the planet, and he had the gall to do it standing on her own front lawn.

She pushed away from Will and faced the developer, squaring off against the man who was, even now, trying to destroy her. How, she didn't care. What mattered was the attempt, the intent, the willpower behind the keyboard. What mattered was her reaction.

Though she'd left her knife in the kitchen, its hilt materialized in her hand, there when she needed it to defend herself from the biggest threat she'd ever faced. Without a single, further thought, she drew back her arm and threw the knife at the developer. It sailed through the air, circling tip over handle, a lazy flash of steel and wood under the bright sun. Four rifles reported, discharging bullets into Alice, and the tip of the knife sliced into the developer's chest and sank deep.

Jack's face whitened around the red ridge of his scar. He shoved his gun aside and caught the developer as he sank to the green, green grass, and gaped at the blood seeping down his vest.

"Holy shit," the developer said.

"Reset!" Jack screamed. "Reset, reset!"

Alice slumped to the floor and smiled as Will hovered over her, cursing her and Jack and the developer and a whole lot of other things she didn't recognize.

Let that be a lesson to them. Let that be something they'd never forget. Alice Humboldt was a woman to be reckoned with. It pleased her no end to discover that about herself, even as life spilled out of her and the world faded to black.

The developer was sitting in the chair beside the hospital bed when Alice's eyes popped open on a life-giving gasp of air.

"Hey," he said.

She narrowed her eyes at him and growled, "You."

He winced. "Yeah, about that. Sorry."

"Sorry," she gritted out. "That's the best you can say for trying to kill me? Sorry?"

He slumped against the back of the chair and his mouth twisted into a sullen frown. "Can't kill what ain't alive."

"I am very much alive, thank you." She huffed and thumped her head into the pillow, and yanked her arms against the manacles chaining her to the bed, rattling them for good measure. "If it looks like a duck, and walks like a duck, and quacks like a duck..."

"Only, you ain't no duck."

"Then what am I?"

"Eh." He scraped a hand over his shaggy auburn hair, ruffling it into a spiky mess. "I don't exactly know."

She aimed a gimlet stare at him. "Do you try to kill every unidentified human you run across?"

"No. No humans." He spread his hands wide, palms up, and shrugged. "Video game characters, sure. It's kinda what I do."

"You should be ashamed of yourself for killing anything."

"Hey, now. You tried to kill me."

"Only because you tried to kill me first."

"I can't believe you're using the self-defense argument," he muttered. "It's not like you're real or anything."

"If it looks like a duck—"

"Ok, ok," he said. "What did you do to Will?"

She widened her eyes, affecting an innocent look. "Who?"

"Oh, geez. Don't try that with me." He lifted one arm toward her and spread his fingers wide, and out of the blue, his tablet appeared in his hand. "It's not like I can't figure it out."

Alice swallowed the knot of fear that popped into her throat, clogging her breath, and bit her tongue. She wouldn't beg. Oh, no, she'd had quite enough of that over the past few weeks, and look where it had gotten her. Chained to a hospital bed talking to a lunatic, that's where. At least Will was passably sane.

"Go away," she said, enunciating every syllable. "Just go back to wherever you came from and leave me alone."

The developer's form shimmied. "Whoa, there."

"Go away." She mustered all her strength and shoved it into the words, adding weight she hadn't known she carried. "Leave me alone."

He held up his hands, his expression panicked. "Wait now, Alice. Let's be reasonable here."

"Go away," she screamed, infusing her voice with all the anger, all the hurt, every ounce of frustration and confusion she'd experienced for as long as she could remember. "Go away!"

The developer's figure shimmied again, and the panic etched into his features morphed into genuine fear. "What the fuck?" he asked, and dissipated into a foggy, amorphous cloud.

Alice flopped back on the bed, her chest heaving under each panted breath. Gradually, the emotions bled out of her, dripping away until her head cleared and her heart calmed.

Her face was wet.

She lifted her hands to dry the tears she hadn't known she was shedding, and was drawn up short. Laughter burst out of her, rebounding around the room. She was still chained to the bed, and as far as she could tell, she'd just sent the only person who could unlock the manacles away.

* * *

Alice woke the next morning, safe and sound in her own bed after hour upon restless hour chained to a hospital bed like a common criminal. She glanced around the room she used to share with John, breathed deeply of the lavender tinged sunshine streaming through the blinds onto the carpet, and exhaled relief into the early morning air. No Developer, thank goodness. What would she have done if he'd returned and followed her home?

She shrugged the question off, sat up, flung the covers off her legs, then sat there staring at her bare knees. If it looked like a duck, it was a duck. She'd been right on that, surely, and the developer quite wrong. She could think and breathe and move and direct her own actions. That made her alive, didn't it? It made her human.

Video game characters.

The developer's words whispered through her mind, eliciting mild nausea in her gut. She cupped her hand over it, tried to will the sick feeling away, but it clung there, scraping away certainty with every thudding heart-beat. No, he wasn't right, couldn't be. She was real, living, human.

But what he said explained an awful lot about her life.

She shrugged the thought away and all but bounced out of bed. Chores. She had chores to do, something a mere character wouldn't do.

Would it?

Doubts lingered in her mind throughout the day, during breakfast and lunch and dinner created with food that didn't quite go together, but she made do. She innovated and improvised, and let pride shore up righteous indignation. Video game characters were tied to a set program, confined by a set of rules they had no hand in developing, unlike her. She made the rules in her life. She chose what to do with her time, how to spend it, whom to marry.

Whom to marry.

She stopped cold in the middle of laying the baby down for bed. John hadn't budged in days. No TV blaring reruns of long-forgotten games late into the night, no beer bottles dripping condensation onto the beeswax finish of the coffee table he'd given her. No bathroom breaks, either, and he hadn't touched a single plate of food she'd set onto a TV tray for him.

Fear gripped her then, as icy in its suddenness as Will's eyes had been the first time he killed her. The way John acted wasn't normal. It wasn't right, wasn't human. How could a man go days or weeks without eating or drinking or even moving?

The answer slapped at her, a sharp agony against her heart. He couldn't. Eventually, a person deprived of food and water died. That's the way it was. Common sense told her that, if not experience.

John wasn't dead.

Alice inhaled slowly, exhaled her fear, or as much of it as she could expel, then gently laid the baby down among soft pink sheets. She stroked a hand over the soft downy head of her only child, then slipped out of the room into the hallway. Down the steps on silent feet, across the living room, and there she was, standing beside her husband.

"How long have we been married?"

She hadn't meant to state her question aloud, hadn't consciously formed it, yet there it was, echoing into the silence, like her. An echo of reality.

No, it couldn't be.

"John," she said, and her voice trembled and shook. "John, honey."

He stared straight ahead, seemingly absorbed in the '70s era baseball game frozen in mid-play on the TV. His expression was blank and his hands were limp on the recliner's arms. A mannequin. The image popped into her head, and instantly, John's features slid away and his hair disappeared, and his head was smooth and round and plastic.

"John!" she screamed. "Look at me, John!"

But he just sat there, a featureless doll dressed in a grown man's clothes, watching America's Pastime as if he were real, as if he were *alive*. And he was supposed to be. He was supposed to be like her, living, breathing, thinking, not a placeholder in the life they'd built together.

Horror joined her fear, rebounding inside her until she was full of terror and loneliness and the shame of knowing she was responsible, somehow, for the condition he was in now. If only she'd tried harder. If only she'd done more, but what? She'd cooked and cleaned and cared for him and the baby and the house, and God knows he hadn't lifted a finger to help her, but he was her husband and she loved him, and she should never have driven him to this lifeless state.

It was all her fault, every bit of it, Will and the bullets and the scarred man and the developer. The food shortage and the fog surrounding the neighborhood and the Volvo breaking down. Every wrong in her world was her fault, *hers*, and now the man she'd married was suffering for it.

"I'm sorry, honey. So sorry."

She sniffed away the tears clogging her sinuses and reached toward him intending to hold him, just hold him for once, something they hadn't done in so long.

Her hand passed right through him.

"John?" she said, and tried again, but he was little more than a ghost or a hologram projected onto the living room floor. She sank down beside him and gave in to the emotions swamping her, and buried her tears in hands as cold as a deep winter's snow.

Alice sat beside John all night, curled up on the living room floor with her arms around her knees and tears seeping out of her eyes. What else could she do? She and John were victims of a sick game. Bob and Lou and...

She dropped her forehead to her knees. Will and his team. Of course they were part of the developer's video game, too, characters caught in an eternal struggle the same way she was.

When the sun crested the horizon (Was it really the sun?), Alice forced herself to get up off the floor, to move. The baby needed her. Even if none of this was real, even if her life was merely a construct of the developer's making, she still felt like a mother. She still felt real, alive.

Human.

The baby was still asleep. Whether because she was programmed that way or because the sun was barely up, what did it matter? The effect was the same.

Alice trudged into her bedroom, picked out clean clothing, stumbled into the bathroom and under the shower. Twenty minutes later, turmoil continued to dog her, but at least she was clean. That was something.

The baby was standing at the railing of her crib when Alice walked back into the nursery. Alice picked her up and cuddled her close, and was rewarded with a hungry mewl and a warm hug.

She smiled and tucked the baby close as she walked downstairs. Motherhood. There was nothing like it.

A loud knock hit the front door, cutting through the baby's growing wail.

Alice froze halfway down the second landing with one foot hanging in the air above the next descending tread and her hands tight on her suddenly too quiet child. Oh, God. If that was the SWAT team, what would she do? She didn't have time to get the baby back into her crib, didn't have time to take her into the kitchen. They always only gave her a few seconds, and then...

"Open up," a hard, male voice called, and Alice nearly wept her relief into the baby's crown.

Will. Maybe he would remember this time. Maybe he would help the baby the way he had before.

Alice glanced at the mannequin that had once been her husband and shook her head. No, not like before, but still. Maybe with Will, there was hope.

She inhaled sharply, exhaled, then walked calmly down the steps and opened the front door. Will was at the lead, as usual, but behind him stood the developer instead of a fully armored SWAT team.

Alice narrowed her gaze on the man who was as responsible for breaking her world as she was, maybe more so. "You."

The developer threw up a hand, palm out, as if he were pleading with her or trying to stop her. "I'm here to help."

She curled herself around the baby and turned sideways, protecting her child as much as she could. "I've seen your brand of help. Truly, I'm not interested."

Will slung his gun over his shoulder. "He hurt you?"

It took everything in her not to scream out an emphatic *yes*. "Not physically, no."

"Some other way then?"

The developer scurried up the stairs onto the front porch. "Wait, no. I didn't do anything except try to fix a bug in my game."

"I'm a bug now, is that it?" Alice huffed. "Is that what we are to you? Bugs?"

"No. I mean." He sighed long and hard, and dropped his hand to his side. "Ok, look. I know this is kinda hard for you to get."

"Oh, I get it, all right. You should see what *getting it* did to my husband."

The developer's face twisted into a confused frown. "Eh?"

"My husband," she repeated, enunciating the syllables, and she pivoted sharply on the ball of one foot and marched toward the recliner where what remained of John sat.

The featureless head drew a sharp pang in her heart. She'd done that, somehow. She'd erased his features, turned him into a lifeless chunk of plastic or whatever he was now, but not on purpose. Never that.

She jerked her chin at the recliner. "There's a bug for you. Why don't you try fixing it this time instead of trying to kill it?"

The developer was already squinting and tapping and fiddling with his tablet. "Hmm. Uh-huh. Wait. No."

Behind the developer, Will shuffled his feet and frowned at her. "You ok?"

"Peachy," she snapped, and immediately regretted it. Will wasn't to blame here. He was just doing his job, a fact he'd reminded her of repeatedly. At least, he was doing the job the developer had assigned him, and she couldn't blame him for that.

She sidled around the developer and stopped beside Will. "Sorry."

"No big. Just, stop crying would you? I can't stand to see a woman cry."

She juggled the baby, swiped at a cheek, and came away with wet fingers. "I didn't realize."

"Yeah, well." He shrugged, jostling the rifle thrown over his shoulder. "You want a tissue or something?"

The developer raised his head and twisted toward them. "You're not programmed for compassion."

Alice almost rolled her eyes, would have if the baby hadn't chosen that moment to revive her fussiness. "He's not programmed to flirt either, but he does."

She stalked out, uncaring if either man followed, and entered the kitchen. There had to be something in here she could give the baby.

Before, there'd been plenty of baby food or, better, she'd cooked fresh vegetables and mashed them up. Now, who knew?

Three doors into her search, Alice hit pay dirt, an entire cabinet full of jars labeled with smiling babies and dancing vegetables. Her relief was so great, it was nearly palpable. She selected two jars and set them on the counter, then snagged a box of baby crackers.

"Need some help?"

Alice whirled around, clutching the baby and the crackers to her chest. "Will! You startled me."

He shrugged. "Figured I could lend a hand while whatsit's working."

"Oh. Sure. Of course. Um." She scurried across the kitchen and retrieved the high chair, settled the baby in it with a minimum of fuss. "Could you open these crackers, please? They should hold her until I can heat up her food."

The developer walked in right then, a deep frown wrinkling his young forehead. "There's a problem with your husband."

"And?" Alice said.

He glanced up at her, blinked. "Why are you feeding the baby? She's not—"

"If you tell me she's not programmed to eat," Alice gritted out, "I will send you back to that rock you crawled out from under."

"Er." His gaze darted from her to the baby to Will and back again. "Right."

"The problem with my husband?"

"That's the problem. It's nothing on my end. Did you do something or something?"

Alice thought back to the night before when she'd been standing there mourning her husband's inactivity, wondering how real her life was, if at all. And John, poor defenseless John.

Will held up a hand. "Ok, that's enough. You're upsetting her."

"But I can't figure this out." The developer waggled his tablet at them. "It's like he's just a placeholder or something. There's not even enough code left to describe him."

Alice's eyes slid shut. A placeholder. Hadn't she been thinking that very thing before John's features slid away? But it had started long before that. As far back as she could remember, he'd been glued to his recliner. She was the one always doing things. She was the one cleaning and cooking and caring for the baby, never him.

Hadn't she lamented that very fact at least a dozen times during the past few months?

She opened her eyes and attempted a wobbly smile for Will's benefit. "It's ok. I'm fine. I just need some...some time, that's all."

"Yeah, ok," he said, though he was frowning too now. "We'll go."

"But I..." the developer said.

Will shot him a hard glance, and the developer swallowed audibly. They left soon after, and Alice was glad. She really did need time to process everything. If not that, then space to simply figure out what she was going to do from here on out, if she could do anything at all.

They came for Alice on a Wednesday morning.

She was in the living room holding a bowl of chicken noodle soup she'd made for her husband. Memorial Day was his favorite holiday. The official start of summer, he'd say, and therefore, grilling season.

John loved nothing better than throwing burgers on the grill.

Uneasiness filled her. No, this was wrong. What had happened to the rest of winter, the start of spring? When had she had time to cook? The last thing she remembered was—

They came for Alice on a Saturday afternoon.

—finding crackers for the baby, and the developer—

They came for Alice on a Friday evening.

—and Will, sweet Will with his beautiful blue eyes and kind heart—

They came for Alice—

"Stop!" she screamed, and the entire world ground to a halt, caught halfway between constructed reality and empty grids of space, like a holodeck on a SciFi TV show stuck between resets.

Her chest heaved under every breath and her mind raced. What was going on? What was happening to her and John and...?

She glanced at him automatically, and reeled back in horror. The mannequin now had features, grotesque eyes and ears and a nose melted into the hard plastic blankness. As she watched, his nose slid into his mouth, or what would've been his mouth. The area there was a jagged, gaping hole above the shifting line of his chin. His fingers twitched against the recliner's arms and his legs ended in stubs just below his knees.

She whirled away, unable to bear the sight of his mangled form. This wasn't her doing. Oh, no. She knew exactly who was to blame for this mess, and she would deal with him soon enough.

But John, poor, dear John who hadn't lifted a finger to help her in ages because he was programmed to sit there day after day, practically glued to the professional sports playing on the TV. He hadn't reacted to her as long as she could remember, which admittedly wasn't a long time, but it was long enough. John wasn't like the baby. He wasn't like Will. There simply wasn't enough substance to his character. What had the developer called it? She searched her memory and finally landed on the word. Code. There wasn't enough code for John to be fully realized, but there could be. She'd changed him from a person to a mannequin. She'd nearly erased his code. If she could do that, surely she could rebuild him again, couldn't she?

She forced herself to turn back around and look at him, to really see him, not as he was now, a drooling, bubbling mess, but as he had been. No, not as he had been. As he *should* have been. The loving husband and father, helpmate and partner, a man in his prime who grilled burgers on Fridays, played Bridge on Saturdays with her and Bob and Lou, and mowed the grass on Sundays. Damn the developer and his game. John should be a real person, like her.

She fixed that vision of him in her head and concentrated hard. John *was* a real person. He had a strong nose and bushy eyebrows and icy blue eyes.

No! That was Will. John's eyes were hazel. Green, gold, and brown all mixed together.

She squinted her eyes together and tried again. Strong nose, bushy eyebrows, hazel eyes. Grilling king, loving father, laughter and endless summer days and long nights making love under the stars.

A thready moan interrupted her. She peeked at John and recoiled. His melting features were dotted now with two noses and four eyes, two hazel and two blue, scrunched together among slashes of thick hair.

Her heart squeezed tight in her chest, then leapt into a panicked gallop. This was all wrong. Maybe if she started with a blank slate...

She thought back to the day she'd accidentally erased his features and imagined him as a placeholder, a lifeless doll. His face obligingly smoothed out even as his back arched off the recliner and a mute scream issued from his throat, muffled by the lack of a mouth.

Oh, God. She was *hurting* him. He was in *pain*, and she was doing it to him.

Enough.

She stepped back, breathed through the panic and hurt and the absolute need to fix this, to make it right, to do anything to return her world to the safe, happy normality it used to be.

No, it had never been normal. It had always been off, wrong even. And it looked like there was nothing she could do to change that. Not like this. Not from the code out, or not with John, at least. Maybe because she wasn't experienced enough, or maybe because there simply wasn't enough code left to work with. Did it matter? In the end, she hadn't been able to reanimate him. She could only bring him pain.

She swiped her hand in an arc between them, mentally erasing everything she'd tried to do. Abruptly, he stilled in the recliner and became once more the limp caricature she'd lived with for so long, minus the human features.

It was time to end this, maybe past time. If the developer wouldn't, then she would. Any wife would do the same rather than allowing her husband to remain an empty shell of a man. That wasn't any kind of life for him. It wasn't any kind of life at all.

"Goodbye, John," she whispered, and with a final shove of her thoughts into the ether, she willed him into nonexistence. He disappeared, leaving the recliner empty and a tad dusty, and she sank down onto the floor and wept for the life they should've had.

They left her alone for a while. She didn't know how long, in spite of gouging little exes into the carving board with the tip of her knife. Those had never disappeared, and now she had long rows of tiny scratches marking the days of her existence.

Why did they remain when so many other elements faded?

She placed her hand over the miserable lump where her heart should've been, if indeed she had one. Poor John. How many other people in her world were like him, mere replicas of humans populating what she'd once thought of as a rich, vibrant life? How many others had the developer sacrificed to his own twisted ends?

Those questions haunted her for days while she waited for him to make another move. After the first two days passed unmolested, she stored the now useless TV in the garage next to the equally decrepit Volvo and rearranged the living room, making room for the baby's playpen which, she admitted, should've been down here all along.

If John had been a more active father, maybe it would've been.

She ignored the pang in her heart, for his absence and for his inherent flaws, flaws he hadn't been able to overcome. How could that be, though? Even accounting for the limited code with which the developer had sketched John, shouldn't he have been able to grow, to question, to test his own boundaries as she did hers? Why had he seemed so unaware of his situation, or so content to remain mired in an endless loop of stale ball-games and warm beer? What made her so different?

Alice paused in the middle of climbing the stairs toward the baby's room, her mind whirling through possibilities. Was she indeed different? What if all of this were simply part of her programming? What if she had been designed to challenge the path laid in front of her?

Was that why her character was a suspected terrorist? Did that explain the seemingly dichotomous nature she possessed within the game, of a mild-mannered wife and mother on one hand, and of a dangerous criminal on the other?

She stood there for a moment, poised between one tread and the next, and pondered the many questions crowding her thoughts. All of them pre-supposed that she was real, an actual person or being, and not merely a figment of the developer's imagination, teased to life within a reality he controlled. Her stomach knotted into a queasy lump. She clenched a fist against her midriff and shook her head. What did it matter if she was real or not? That she was standing there questioning her own existence, that she could, to some limited degree, control that existence proved that she was more than the developer had intended her to be. If she was, then perhaps she could outgrow him. Perhaps she could affect the outcome of the game, the world, or whatever this place she inhabited was.

But how?

She shook her head again and continued up the stairs. *How* could come later. Right now, she had a baby to tend and supper to fix, and that was more than enough to occupy her time for the foreseeable future.

A hard fist banged on the front door, interrupting Alice and the baby's midmorning playtime. She sighed and put the baby down on the quilt spread across the living room floor. Now what?

The banging picked up, accompanied by a shouted, "Open up!"

Alice's heart skipped a beat and acquired an oddly happy thrill. That had sounded like Will, and there was only one reason he could be out there.

Which begged the question as to why she was smiling.

She forced her mouth into a frown as she stood, walked to the door, and opened it. Sure enough, there was Will decked out in his usual SWAT gear. The porch was empty behind him, and his gun was held low across his body.

"What's wrong?" she asked.

"They're coming." Will glanced over his shoulder, then adjusted his flat black helmet. "Look, I shouldn't be here."

She nodded, then shook her head. "Why are you here?'

His icy blue eyes fixed on her and his shoulders relaxed. Slowly, his mouth curled into a wicked smile, heating his gaze, and she blushed from the top of her head to the tips of her toes and everywhere in between.

"Cut it out," she said, and almost added a tart *I'm married* before the memory of John's virtual death intruded, slicing grief and helplessness through the happiness of Will's presence.

Will's grin faded. He cupped a hand over her shoulder and squeezed. "What is it?"

She shook her head again. How could she possibly explain the past few days or weeks or whatever unit of time she was confined to? At last she managed a weak, "Nothing."

His expression twisted into a skeptical frown and his hand dropped away, leaving her shoulder cold without his heat warming her. "If you don't want to talk about it..."

She did want to talk about it, and right now, he was about the only friend she had, or the closest thing to it.

"No, it's just—" She sighed and managed a wobbly smile. "Maybe we could talk later, once your team makes their sweep."

"Sounds good." His gaze slipped past her for the briefest moment, then returned to her, softer somehow. "How's the baby?"

"She's doing good. I think a new tooth is popping up."

"Teething," he said, and shared a grin with her. "I'd better get back to it."

"Sure," she agreed, then closed her mouth around an awkward realization that the next time she saw him, he'd probably kill her.

Will's next visit played out almost exactly like every other raid his SWAT team made on her house, or close enough. He banged on her door, demanding entrance. She opened it and protested her innocence, and the next thing she knew, a bullet slammed into her and the world faded to black.

The whole episode felt like a play, scripted from beginning to end, she thought after waking in her bed surrounded by the last of the day's sunlight shining through the window. In a way, it was, if the developer could be believed.

She heaved a sigh as she slung the covers off her legs and slid out of bed. Who was she kidding? Belief had formed a long time ago. No use denying it any longer.

The baby's laughter drifted to her, and in a panic, Alice raced downstairs. As soon as her feet hit the living room's floor, she stumbled to a halt. There sat Will on the quilt she'd spread out earlier, lifting the baby over his head.

Alice uttered a soft, "Oh!"

Will tucked the baby against his broad chest and twisted around. "I let myself in."

"I see."

"Hope you don't mind, but when I doubled back and you didn't answer..."

He shrugged, then turned his attention back to the baby and swung her up in the air over his head. The baby squealed a delighted shriek and clapped her hands against Will's cheeks.

They looked so comfortable with each other.

Alice crossed the living room and sat down on the opposite side of the quilt. "How long have you been here?"

"Long enough to change a diaper and figure out where the baby snacks are." He smacked a kiss to the baby's cheek, then handed her over to Alice. "Listen, about earlier—"

She cut him off with a firm shake of her head. "You're just doing your job, but maybe next time you could let somebody else shoot me."

Will's gaze swung up and he huffed out a humorless laugh. "Don't be so cavalier about it. You might not come back one day."

"I always have." Though she wasn't stupid enough to believe she always would. "What time is it?"

"About seven. Why?"

"Hungry?"

That cocksure grin flashed. "Always."

She handed the baby back to him. "Come on then. I'll make supper, unless you're expected elsewhere."

"No," he said simply. "I just have one question. What's her name?"

Alice paused in the act of pushing herself off the floor. The baby had always been just that, the baby, no name, no identity of her own. Alice had never questioned it before, never once realized that her own child lacked something so basic.

She leaned over and brushed a kiss over the baby's cheek, and in that moment, the name came to her as if it had always been. "Sarah," she said softly. "Her name is Sarah."

Will jiggled a grinning Sarah in his arms. "A good name."

Yes, it was, Alice thought, and marveled at the calm assurance settling over her.

It became easier to track time after that. A few days after Will's visit, one month rolled into another. The calendar pinned to the kitchen wall reflected the change without Alice having to lift a finger to flip the pages. She discovered it one morning while waiting for the baby to wake up. A field of mown hay had replaced the bright petals of a single sunflower decorating the eggshell colored wall.

October was upon them, and with it Halloween. She tapped a finger against the square enclosing the last day of the month and smiled as she mentally created a list. Decorations for the house, candy for visitors, a costume for Sarah, maybe even one for herself, and trick-or-treating around the neighborhood.

She hadn't ventured out in a long while, not since John's death at least. Maybe it was time she sought out some fresh air, reconnected with her neighbors, even if they weren't real.

A soft knock hit the front door, then it creaked open and Will called, "Hello?"

Alice's heart flipped over. She tightened her bathrobe over the butterflies fluttering in her stomach as she hurried into the living room. Will was just visible through the gap in the front door. She waved him in and said, "Don't tell me your team is about to do a sweep. I haven't even had coffee yet."

He pushed the door open and stepped inside. "You've got coffee?"

When she got a good look at him, she skittered to a halt. He was wearing a form-fitting, black Metallica t-shirt over khaki cargo shorts and carried an olive green duffel bag in one hand.

It was the first time she'd seen him out of his SWAT gear.

Alice patted a hand over her errant heart, attempting to calm it. Will was handsome in his police outfit, but in civilian clothing, he was devastating. His dark hair was ruffled, as if he'd just risen from bed, and his shoulders seemed even broader under the simple t-shirt. She deliberately fixed her gaze on his downturned face, refusing to glance at the bare, muscled legs showing below his shorts, all too aware of her unkempt hair and the too large t-shirt she wore under her robe.

Thank goodness she'd taken the time to brush her teeth before coming downstairs.

"I was about to put some on," she said. "What's in the bag?"

"My gear." He dropped the duffel on the floor just inside the living room and shut the door. "In case I'm called out while I'm here."

He said it like that was something she should know, or maybe that was her imagination. She pivoted on a bare foot and walked back into the kitchen. Since he was here, she might as well enjoy the company.

As part of her overall plan to socialize more, not because he was easy on the eyes and easier to be around.

"Breakfast?" She swung the refrigerator door open and peered inside at the shelves packed exactly as they should be. "I can make bacon and eggs or—"

Will's arms came around her from behind and drew her against his hard body.

Alice's breath froze in her lungs, choking her ability to speak. What was he doing holding her like that, as if they were a couple, and not killer and killee?

"Why don't I take you and Sarah out tonight?" he said. "I know this place downtown. Best pasta in the city, kid-friendly tables."

She eased away from him on the pretext of pulling out the milk. "That's not necessary."

His hands tightened on her hips, keeping her right where she was. "It's the least I can do. You're all the time cooking for me."

"Just once," she murmured, and that not a full week past.

Ha laughed against her hair. "We've been dating for weeks now, baby. Am I that forgettable?"

He wasn't, but that wasn't the point.

"I'm married," she said.

Will stiffened behind her and his fingers dug into her skin through her robe. "What? When did that happen?"

Alice turned in his arms, a quart of milk held in front of her as if it were a shield. "About five years ago, give or take. You met him once.

Don't you remember?"

One corner of his mouth turned down in a frown.

When he didn't say anything, she rushed on. "Not long ago. Your team came by and it was just John and Sarah. You brought her playpen downstairs, then came to see me in the hospital?"

"No, I—" He grimaced, closed his bright eyes tight. "What the hell?"

"You ok?"

"Yeah. Just a headache." He rubbed the heels of his hands into his eyes as he backed up a step. "Kinda sudden. For a minute there, I could almost see this guy sitting in a recliner in front of a TV watching a game or something."

"That's it."

She set the milk down on the counter and guided Will to a barstool tucked under the kitchen island's lip. A growing whimper drifted through the baby monitor. Sarah was awake. Great timing, that.

Alice patted Will's shoulder and said, "Be right back."

"Bring some aspirin down when you come?" he said, and she nodded as she hustled out of the room and upstairs.

Sarah was wet and cranky. Alice took a few minutes to change her diaper and calm her down, then grabbed a bottle of pain killer out of the bathroom and hurried back down the stairs toward the kitchen.

It was empty.

"Will?" she said. "Where are you?"

The house remained quiet. She grabbed a teething cookie and handed it to Sarah as she searched the first floor. No one was there. Alice glanced in the living room, searching for his bag, but it was gone, too. In a mild panic, she opened the front door and scanned the street.

"Everything ok?" a familiar male voice called.

Alice glanced across her yard and around a giant oak that hadn't been there the last time she'd been outside. "We're fine, Bob. Just thinking about taking a walk."

"Great day for it," he said. "Hey, Lou wanted me to ask if you and Will would like to go to the movies with us on Saturday night. One of her nieces can babysit, if you can't find a sitter."

Wait, how did Bob know Will? And since when did Lou have nieces?

"It's ok if you've already got plans," Bob added. "We can do it another time, or maybe play some Rummy."

She shook the questions away. "A movie is probably fine."

"Great. Gotta get to work."

He waved and got in his car. Alice lifted her hand in a half-hearted wave, then retreated into her home and leaned her back against the closed front door. First Will and now Bob. What was next? Would John magically return to life? Would the fog shrouding the edges of the neighborhood beyond the brand new tree line suddenly dissipate? Or would everything begin disappearing like it had before, when the developer had tried to "fix" her?

She narrowed her eyes even as her arms tightened around Sarah. The developer. Ten to one, he had his fingers in this pie, and that wouldn't do at all.

Alice spent the day mulling over the situation while going about the routine she'd established for Sarah since naming her. The longer she mulled, the madder she got, and the madder she got, the more determined she was to stop the developer once and for all.

How she was going to stop him was another matter entirely.

At Sarah's naptime, and after considerable thought, Alice picked up the kitchen phone's handset and dialed zero.

"Operator," a cheery voice intoned.

"Would you connect me with the developer, please?" Alice asked.

"Certainly! Please hold."

Tinny muzak filtered through the line. Alice propped her back against the wall and patiently waited. A few minutes later, the muzak cut out and a male voice said, "Greg Benson."

Tentatively, she asked, "Is this the developer?"

"Yeah, I'm a game developer."

Relief flooded through her. Calling him had actually worked. Amazing.

"Mr. Benson," she said, "this is Alice. Alice Humboldt?"

Something loud banged on the other end of the line and Greg yelped out a mangled, "What?"

"Alice Humboldt. From the game you're making?"

"Alice Hum..." He dragged the first syllable of her name into a long *hmm*. "How the hell did you get my number? Wait, scratch that. How the hell did you call me on my friggin cellphone from inside a video game?"

"Er," she said, and since she really didn't know, she pushed ahead with her reason for calling. "I want you to put Will back the way you found him."

"What?"

A brilliant idea hit and she nearly laughed. "And put John back in the game. I don't care if he can only watch TV, but it'd be nice if he sometimes played with Sarah, too."

"Sarah?"

"Yes, Sarah," Alice said as patiently as she could. "My daughter?"

"Oh, right. When did you...? Never mind. What's wrong with Will?"

"He's not right. This morning he came by and acted like he'd never met John. And he wanted to take me and Sarah out for dinner!"

"I wish somebody'd take me out for dinner," the developer muttered.

Maybe if he didn't have people in his game shoot innocent housewives, he'd get a date.

She wisely kept that opinion to herself and pressed onward. "I know you did something to him. Fix it."

"Heh. Ok, look." His sigh shot static through the line connecting them. "I was doing a last-minute debugging of the game. We're on the verge of beta testing."

"I don't know what that means."

"It means we're... Never mind. That's not important. What's important is that I noticed some glitches in the game that weren't supposed to be there."

"Glitches," she said flatly.

"Not you. I mean, you I can't get rid of. You're in everything. Which won't mean a thing to you." He muttered something under his breath, too low for her to hear, then continued. "What I'm saying is, some of the characters have been affected."

"Affected how?"

"They're gone. Disappeared. That's why I changed Will up a bit, gave him a new back story, inserted a love interest. I figured, you know. Since he kinda liked you, it'd be, you know."

She banged the back of her head against the kitchen wall and stared up at the ceiling. "No, I don't know. Why don't you explain?"

"It's like this. I can't add any more characters to the game."

"Why not?"

"Because I don't control that part of the game anymore." His voice was suddenly too gentle, too kind. "I can fix Will, no problem. That's just a little rewinding, but adding back a character that's been deleted? No can do."

Sorrow welled up inside her, overflowing into tears. She sniffed them away, swiped the back of her hand across her face, and tried to talk around the tightness in her throat. "I killed him."

"No, no," the developer said. "You didn't kill him. I mean, you can't kill what doesn't exist, and he didn't exist, not the way you did. Do. Are."

"So you can't help him."

"It's not that I don't want to. Have you tried?"

"Yes, I have."

"And?"

"It didn't go well."

"Ah." He sighed again, eliciting more static, then a sharp rat-a-tat-tat of fingers on keyboards sounded. "Look, we're going into beta any day now. Can you just...hold off on doing anything about John for a while?"

The image of her husband's body contorted in agony popped into her head. "I'm not going to try to bring him back."

"Ok, good. Whew. Look, I know he was your husband and all, but..." A loud smack of flesh on flesh came through the line. "What am I saying? You're a character in a game."

Maybe to him she was. "I feel real."

"Heh. Well. Nothing I can do about that."

"Don't kill me." The words came out thin and weak, not at all the way she'd meant them to.

"Delete," he corrected. "Don't worry. I won't. Can't anyway. We've put too much effort into this game, and way too much money. It's just going to have to run the way it is."

"Except for Will," she prompted.

"Yeah, of course. I'm already on that." He cleared his throat, coughed. "Look, if you need anything, just, I don't know. Call me again? Maybe we can work something out where you don't ruin the game. Ha, ha. Don't want to lose my job or anything."

"I'll try," she said, but it was a muted promise at best. What could she really do from inside a game? The few things she'd tried had backfired. Well, what she'd tried to do for John had backfired. She'd managed a few things well, or the developer wouldn't have tried so hard to stay on her good side.

They exchanged wary goodbyes, and she hung up as she replayed the conversation in a futile search for meaning.

Will's team showed up on her doorstep three days later. His eyes had that hard, icy gleam they'd held the first time she'd met him and his expression was an iron mask under the black gleam of his helmet.

Her heart sank in her chest. The developer had rewound Will too far, right back to the beginning. Her hands tightened into fists at her side. It wasn't fair. The one real friend she had, the one person she could talk to, was gone, replaced by this unfeeling automaton hellbent on destroying her.

Her eyes narrowed on his team, and the hard fury, the frustration and helplessness, every bad thing that had ever happened to her coalesced into a pinpoint of determination.

They wanted to kill her? Fine. Let them try.

She whirled around and raced through the house, ignoring the shouts of angry male voices and the thud of booted feet onto her freshly mopped floor. The knife. If she could just get to it, she could—

A firm arm wrapped around her waist from behind and lifted her off the ground, dragging her backward toward the door.

"No," she screamed, and kicked and beat at the man holding her.

"Fuck, lady, we just wanna talk," Will said against her ear, but she was too far gone to hear him. She threw her head back hard, hit something that hurt like hell, and was satisfied by the low male curse rumbling against her ear.

That'd teach him to revert on her, just when she was starting to trust him.

His arm tightened around her middle and he heaved her backward. She clutched it, still fighting, and hurt fury radiated out of her, touching everything in its path. Why had he had to change? Why couldn't he just be Will, her friend who came by and played with Sarah? Will, who warned her before his team struck? Will, who wanted her to come back every time she was killed?

He stopped dead still, and his arm trembled against her ribs. "Alice?"

She sagged against him, limp as a ragdoll under the hope surging through her misery. "Will?"

"What's going on? I—"

"What the fuck?" a familiar male voice barked, and Will swung toward it, taking Alice with him. There stood Jack, his scarred face twisted into a scowl. "What are you doing, Will?"

Will raised his rifle and pointed it straight at Jack. "What I should've done a long time ago."

Will shifted Alice to the side, and the rifle discharged, kicking hard into Will's shoulder, hard enough for Alice to feel it.

Jack staggered back and a red splotch blossomed along his stomach. "What the hell?" he murmured, then everything went black as abruptly as the snuffing of a candle.

The mattress dipped, waking Alice from a deep sleep, and a large, warm body curled around her. Her eyes flew open and she stiffened in the darkness shrouding her bedroom.

"Relax," Will said. He nuzzled the side of her throat, settled her hips more firmly against his. "Sunrise is still hours away. We've got time."

Alice twisted around in his loose grip, facing him. "What are you doing in my bed?"

"Sleeping. Too tired for anything else."

"No, I mean—"

His arm tightened around her, bringing her square against his bare chest. "Cut me some slack, Alice. It's been a rough day. Almost got fired for shooting the squad leader."

Her mouth snapped shut. "You remember that?"

"Kinda hard to forget the ass chewing I got." Will yawned, touched a kiss to her forehead. "Mmm. You smell good. New shampoo?"

"Same one," she said faintly, then tentatively tacked on, "Have you, um, slept with me before?"

"First time. You blacked out earlier, and I didn't want to leave Sarah alone. Lou took care of her while I worked, then I came back to check on you and..." His shoulder lifted and fell against her. "Have to be back here first thing for work. Seemed kinda silly to go home for the night."

"Oh."

His hand slid up and down her arm, then landed on her hip and squeezed. "No couch, no spare bedroom."

The abrupt change of topic lost her. "What?"

"I'm not sleeping on the floor."

"Oh. Right. I'll see about getting a couch."

"Not on my account." He pressed his hips into hers, rubbing a firm erection against her stomach, and a low laugh rumbled through his chest. "Kinda like where I'm at."

"Will, please."

"Mmm. I love it when you beg."

She huffed out a sigh against his chest. "I thought you were too tired for anything but sleep."

"Never too tired for sex, baby." He found her hand and pressed it flat against the slow thud of his heartbeat, and held it there with his own. "How long has it been since your husband died?"

The question shot through her, startling her. How long had it been since she'd thought of John, other than to regret to way he'd died, or to wish he'd been created better?

Will brushed another kiss across her forehead. "Hey, sorry. I didn't mean to push."

"You weren't."

"He just hasn't been here for a while."

"Weeks," she murmured. Months maybe. She had no way to tell, no way to measure the time since John's death except by the sorrow of mourning. Oddly, it was a thin thread in her heart, dwarfed by lingering guilt. Had she really thought so little of her husband, or was the lack, like everything else, merely a byproduct of a manufactured existence?

"And I've kinda got a thing for sexy single moms."

She leaned away from Will and studied his features in the room's shadows, what she could make out. His eyes were closed, but a faint smile curved his mouth. "Thanks for taking care of Sarah."

"Couldn't leave her." He tucked her against his chest, rested his chin on the top of her head, and relaxed around her. "G'night, Alice."

"Goodnight, Will."

She held still against him, listening to him breathe, and measured the beat of his heart against her palm. Will was half-naked in her bed. Laughter bubbled up, threatening to spill, and she tamed it by burying her face in his chest. His scent tickled her nose, sharply masculine. Soap, maybe?

She shook her head and relaxed against him. It wouldn't hurt to sleep with him tonight, just sleep. Tomorrow she'd figure out how to get a couch, the kind that pulled out into a bed. Spare sheets, too, or did she have some stashed away in a linen closet somewhere? She yawned and curled her fingers into a loose fist against his chest, and slid into sleep.

Alice slipped out of bed the next morning, leaving Will sprawled across the beige cotton sheets. Sometime in the middle of the night, he'd shifted onto his back, and she'd ended up plastered all over him with her arm thrown across his chest and one leg over his thighs.

Which is when she'd discovered he wasn't half-naked, but completely nude.

She tried washing away the heat that discovery had created within her under the hot spray of a shower, and failed miserably. What was it about Will anyway? Any sane woman would've kicked him out a long time ago, say, right about the first time he shot her.

Obviously, she wasn't sane, but whatever. Nobody was perfect.

She dressed quickly in cargo pants and an athletic top, checked on Sarah, who was still sleeping soundly, and bounced quietly down the stairs, humming a tuneless melody. Breakfast. It was the least she could do for him after he'd taken care of Sarah while Alice was out cold. She had to find a way to fix that.

Maybe the developer would know how.

She shook her head as she opened the fridge and surveyed its contents. What did Will like? Eggs, bacon? No, she could do better than that, and set to cooking blueberry muffins, a light fruit salad, and a Mexican breakfast casserole.

Half an hour later, Will entered the kitchen holding Sarah. "Look what I found."

Alice half turned away from the cantaloupe she was cubing and smiled at him. "I could've gotten her."

"I was already up there."

He set Sarah in her highchair and adjusted the lap straps. His muscles bulged and flexed under the thin, tight-fitting black shirt he wore. Alice's heart flipped over and that traitorous heat slithered through her. She whirled around and busied herself with the fruit. John was dead and had been for a while, true, but that didn't mean she was ready to throw herself at the first eligible bachelor who slid into her bed in the middle of the night.

Will's hands cupped her hips and his face nuzzled the side of her throat. "Good morning."

She risked glancing at him over her shoulder. His expression was oddly shuttered. "Good morning. Did you sleep well?"

"Mmm." His mouth curved into a faint smile. "Your hands wandered a little last night."

Heat flooded her cheeks. "I'm so sorry."

"Don't be. I liked it. Next time, mine may wander, too." He turned her all the way toward him and gently pried the knife and fruit out of her hands, and when he looked at her, his blue eyes were hot and a little wild under the sweep of his lashes. "I've been wanting to do this for a long time."

The softly murmured words swept over her, but before she could absorb them, his hands cupped her face and his mouth came down on hers, gentle as a leaf floating on the wind, and he was kissing her, coaxing her into pleasure with the soft rub of his lips against hers.

She wrapped her hands around his wrists and melted into his kiss, opening for him, reveling in the sweetness of his touch. How long had it been since a man had kissed her? Try as she might, she couldn't remember, couldn't recall even one kiss from her husband. The knife, yes, and all the other gifts he'd given, but a kiss?

Never.

The thought startled her, and she stiffened. Will drew away from her, gradually ending the kiss, and touched his forehead to hers. "Too soon?"

She shook her head once. "No. It was nice."

"Nice?" He huffed out a laugh. "Hell, woman. What's a man gotta do?"

The oven's timer dinged, and right on cue, Sarah smacked her hands against the highchair's tray. Alice stood on her tiptoes and brushed a tentative kiss across Will's mouth, and scooted away when he reached for her. "Breakfast."

He followed her and trapped her against the counter as she was reaching for oven mitts, his hands braced against the counter on either side of her torso. His hips pressed into hers and his eyes lingered on her lips. "You can't run forever, baby."

Sarah let out a gibbering string of nonsense, and Will let Alice go. She retrieved the casserole from the oven with shaky hands and finished preparing the meal, but his words echoed in her mind, both a warning and a promise.

Will left after breakfast and a warning as to what time he expected his team to arrive at Alice's house. "Leave Sarah at Lou's, ok? I worry about her when we conduct a raid."

"Then don't do it," Alice said tartly, and he grinned and yanked her into a hard kiss that left her reeling long after he was gone.

He was right. Sarah wasn't safe here when his team came a-calling, so Alice bundled her daughter up and carried her across the lawn stretching between their house and their neighbor's, and begged a favor of Lou.

"'Course I'll keep this little angel, and I'll spoil her rotten," Lou said.

"Cards Saturday night?"

Alice kissed her daughter goodbye. "I'll ask Will."

"He's quite the young man." Lou narrowed her brown eyes behind the bifocals perched on the tip of her round nose. "Is he sticking around?"

A blush heated Alice's cheeks, and Lou cackled and took Sarah, leaving Alice with no excuse to linger.

Will's team arrived right on schedule. Alice dutifully played her part, and was completely unsurprised when Jack himself shot her this time.

Imagine that. One of their visits ending in her getting shot.

She came to still lying where they'd left her, sprawled across her living room floor, and pushed herself upright, frowning. Will should've been back by now, unless...

She opened the front door. The sun had barely moved across the sky, as far as she could tell. Maybe she hadn't been out that long.

She straightened her clothes, checked for bullet holes or bloodstains, and was relieved when she found none. That was one thing she could count on, anyway. Her clothing escaped unscathed from these little incidents, even if she didn't.

A late model, full-sized truck pulled into her driveway and parked, and Will stepped out, his dark hair sticking up in a dozen different directions. "Hey. Didn't expect you to be awake."

Alice stepped onto the porch and shut the front door, then bopped down the steps toward him. "How long was I out?"

"Not long. A couple of hours maybe." He met her halfway and swung her into a hug. "Sorry about Jack. He was pissed 'cause I shot him."

"Still?" She pursed her lips into a bow, hiding her humor. It was past time Jack was on the receiving end of a bullet. If Will hadn't done it, maybe she would've, eventually, when she got fed up with being their scapegoat. "I was just about to pick up Sarah."

Will's grin turned into a playful leer. "Wanna go back inside and take advantage of having a babysitter for a while?"

"If you wanted sex, you shouldn't have shot me that first time, and then a second and a third." She huffed out her exasperation and stepped away from him. "Really, Will. Couldn't you find a way to stop shooting me? I get tired of blacking out every time the game resets."

The grin slipped from his face, and a frown grew in its place. "What game?"

"This game. You know." She held her hands out and twirled in a slow circle. "The video game we're in? Me suspected bad guy, you part of the hero squad?"

"This isn't a game, Alice. It's life." He ran both hands over his hair, mussing it even more. "Where did you get a crazy idea like that anyway?"

"From the developer."

"The who?" He cocked his head to the side and a dangerous gleam entered his eyes. "Are you seeing somebody else?"

She sputtered out a laugh. "What? No! Of course not. The developer is the guy who created this game, that's all."

"It's not a game," Will repeated, the words harder, heavier. "Why do you keep saying that?"

"Because it's true. Oh, Will." She sighed and searched for a way to help him understand. "Haven't you ever wondered why your team does the same routine every time it's out? Searches the same houses, looks for the same people?"

He shook his head slowly. "That's my job, Alice. We've talked about this before."

"Yes, honey, it is your job, but—" She shook her head and placed one palm flat against his chest. "If we were real, how could I still be alive after you shot me? Jack shot me this afternoon. Look."

She tried to take his hand so he could feel the smoothness of her chest, but he shook his head and backed away from her, nearly stumbling in his hurry to get away.

"No. It's real, this thing I feel, here." He thumped a fist against his chest. "I'm half in love with you, Alice. How can that not be real?"

"It is," she said gently, and slowly unbuttoned her shirt. If he wouldn't touch her, then she'd just have to show him. "For us, it's real, but we're characters, Will, just characters in a game."

She finished unbuttoning her shirt and held the sides wide, baring herself to him, thankful school was still in session so the neighborhood kids couldn't tattle on her for flashing her bra.

Will stared at her as the color leached from his face and he sank to his knees on the concrete sidewalk bisecting her yard. "No. It can't be."

"Will—"

His body flickered in and out of existence, and raw panic shot through her.

"Will!" she screamed, and scrambled toward him. Not Will, no, please, not him, not after John died. She couldn't take it, couldn't lose him, too, not now.

"Alice." His voice faded in and out, in time with his flickering form. "Al...I...not—"

She dropped down in front of him and wrapped herself around him. "Stay with me, Will. This is real, I swear, me and you and Sarah. We're real. You have to believe me."

"Alice," he whispered, and the desperation rose so sharply in her, she acted without thinking. She cupped her hands behind his head and drew him down, and kissed him, shoving every ounce of her own belief into the kiss on the thin hope that he'd accept what they had, here in this little slice of a video game, accept it and her, and understand that it didn't matter, nothing else mattered but the friendship and family they were creating between them.

His arms came around her. Slowly, he returned her kiss, and finally, after long moments of doubt and praying to a god she wasn't sure existed, Alice broke the kiss and hugged him close.

"I'm sorry," he said, one palm holding the back of her head to his chest. "I'm so sorry, baby. Shh, don't cry. I'm here."

But there was nothing for it. Alice clutched him tightly as tears overflowed down her cheeks, and she sobbed all her worry into his chest as he held her and whispered softly to her that he'd never leave her again.

After the storm of tears passed, Alice slipped into the downstairs bathroom and washed her face while Will retrieved his duffel and took a shower upstairs. She busied herself with housework while she waited for him to finish.

Laundry. It never ended. She gathered her and Sarah's dirty clothes, dumped them into the washing machine in the tiny room off the garage, and stood there staring down at the half full tub, her thoughts in a turmoil.

She'd almost lost Will again today, almost lost him to the sheer reality of their existence. How could he not have known? But no, he was a police officer, a former soldier. He wouldn't have questioned his situation, necessarily, not unless some conflict arose as it had today.

What if she hadn't been able to hold onto him? What if her being there hadn't been enough?

She shook her worry off and carried the empty laundry basket upstairs without starting the wash. There was enough room in the machine for Will's clothes. No sense wasting water on half a load when she could take care of all of it in one fell swoop.

When she entered her bedroom, he was sitting on the edge of her bed dressed in boxer briefs, his hair damp and wild from the shower.

She set the laundry basket aside and sat down beside him. "You ok?"

"Yeah, sure." He leaned his forearms against his bare thighs and hung his head. "I can't believe I fell apart like that."

"Will," she said.

"All I could think about was you." He huffed out a laugh and rubbed a hand across his nape. "I kept thinking, Alice is real, she's so real, but there you were, showing me your chest. Not a scar, not a scratch, and you were right. You're still alive and you shouldn't be."

She searched for something to say, something comforting or wise, and came up empty. "I'm sorry," she said instead.

"Don't be. I'm glad you told me. Now I know. I mean, so much makes sense now." He sat up, hands on his thighs, and stared at the bedroom wall, his expression inscrutable. "Why didn't I see it before?"

"Stop," she said, but the word was easy, gentle. "Stop beating yourself up. You're not to blame here."

"But I perpetuated it. If it's just a game, I could've stopped—" He heaved a sigh and finally, at last, looked at her. "I've never fallen apart like that before, not once. Not under heavy fire, not when a perp coked out. I'm sorry."

"You keep saying that."

She attempted a wobbly smile and slid a hand across the bare skin of his back, over solid muscle and strong bones and the good heart of a man who'd done the best he could in spite of what he believed her to be. A terrorist. God, couldn't the developer have come up with a better scenario?

"I need to get Sarah," she said.

"Yeah?" He leaned toward her, the ghost of a smile lingering around his mouth. "When did you tell Lou you'd be over there?"

"I didn't know how long it would take, so—"

He launched himself toward her and tackled her onto the bed, and his eyes were that rough combination of hot and wild she was beginning to love.

"So we've got a little while, huh?" he asked.

"Will, come on."

"Yeah, I think I'll work on coming on." He settled himself against her and dipped his head, brushed a kiss against her mouth and drew back. "I need you, Alice. Tell me you need me, too."

"I do, Will." She laughed, surprised at the certainty of her words and the emotions swirling through her. She needed him, just once. Maybe she always had. "Kiss me."

"Once I start, I may not stop."

"Don't," she said, and he lowered his head and kissed her, and he didn't stop until the wild heat he gave so willingly burst over them both in a satisfying rush of pleasure and warmth and need.

Alice rested her head on Will's chest and drew random circles with her fingertip over his heart. It pounded under her ear, matching the thready rhythm of her own heart. Sex with Will had been wonderful, amazing, and incredibly eye opening.

"Thank you," she said.

His hand smoothed up and down her arm where he held her. "For what?"

"You know."

"I do?"

She ignored the humor underscoring his question and pressed a tentative kiss to his chest. For everything they'd just done, their relationship was still fresh, shiny, like a newly minted copper penny.

Will's sigh feathered against her forehead. "Where do we go from here?"

"What do you mean?"

"I'm a police officer, you're a suspected terrorist." His shoulder shifted, jostling her, and his hand curled around her arm. "Not the best foot to start off on."

"We'll work it out."

"I know."

The implicit faith in his voice warmed her. As her belief had saved him, maybe his would save her, too.

"I want to take you and Sarah and run until you're both safe."

"I wish you could."

She buried her face in his chest and slid her leg up and over his thighs. God, did she ever wish it could be that easy, but even here in Gameville, nothing ever was. The developer had assigned each of them their roles. He'd said they were set, that there was nothing he could do to change them, and that was her fault. Somehow she'd overtaken the system, the character end anyway. If any changes were going to be made, it was up to her to make them.

It would be easier if she could figure out how she was affecting the game, and why she'd grown to be such a crucial part of it.

Maybe in time, she'd understand, but for now, she was content with where she was, here in this bed with Will.

Finally, she said, "I think they'll find us wherever we go."

"Then we need to prepare." He cupped her face and tilted it toward his, and kissed her, his lips tender against hers. "I want you to start working out with me, training. I can show you how to use that knife of yours, or I can get you a gun and we can go to the range."

The knife would be better, at least until Sarah was old enough to understand the dangers of firearms. It had gotten Alice through some tough times and had often been the only thing she could count on, especially in the days when life had gotten a little scary.

"I can't leave Sarah with Lou a lot, though," she said. "I don't want someone else raising my daughter, and Lou has a life of her own."

"There's a childcare center near the gym. Half an hour a day, maybe an hour. Is that doable?"

"I think I can stand to be away from her that long every day."

He laughed and rolled on top of her, and settled himself between her thighs. "I have a confession."

She arched an eyebrow. "Oh?"

"I lied to you."

"About what?"

"I'm not half in love with you. I haven't been since the day I thought you were going to turn the Volvo into a bomb. There's just something about you, baby."

He dipped his head and kissed her, and spent a long time showing her exactly how full of love he was.

Three months later

Alice twisted her hair into a braid and secured it with a rubber band. Will was in the shower getting ready for work, same as her. That they were on opposite sides of a manufactured conflict had done not a thing to stifle their deepening love.

She dropped the braid and let her hand fall to the tiny his and her boxes sitting side by side on top of the vanity he'd bought her when he'd moved in two weeks ago. Wedding rings, for the day when they would officially celebrate the start of their life together. He'd been all for doing the deed the minute he'd proposed. She'd wanted to wait until after the New Year. They'd compromised, of course, and set a date just a month away with the end of the year still two months beyond that.

They'd become good at compromising.

She smiled and tapped the boxes a final time, then slipped on the clothes she'd picked out for today's raid, an echo of the clothes Will would put on after his shower. A black, form-fitting athletic top, black cargo pants, and ankle high combat boots.

The developer had helped Alice figure out how to control the game, to some extent, through phone calls and emails. She'd practiced first on inanimate objects and somehow managed to conjure up that sleeper couch for company without having to order one from the furniture store in town. When she was certain she'd do no harm, she'd moved on to the stand in characters filling the game's landscape, fleshing them out until they seemed real to anyone on the outside.

Just yesterday, Greg had told her the early reviews for the game were outstanding. Everyone was raving over how realistic it was, down to the tiniest detail. Will had helped there. His knowledge of combat systems had been much deeper than the developer's thanks to an info dump of military history and arms that Greg had loaded into Will's character files when he was creating Will, information Greg had never delved deeply into on his own.

Much of the realism was due to Alice's input and manipulation of the game itself, and the unpredictable variability a sentient artificial intelligence brought to the game. That's what the developer had called her, and he'd said it with such pride she didn't have the heart to tell him she was still in her virtual infancy.

The game was such a hit, there was talk of a sequel, but Greg was stalling. He hadn't figured out how to replicate Alice, and she was happy where she was, in this game with Will and Sarah and the life they were creating.

And it was a life. Even the developer agreed and had long ago started calling them people instead of characters. He'd helped her install a computer interface in the kitchen between his world and hers, and she was learning everything she could from him. The outside world pressed in on her, the Internet, Greg called it, an amorphous presence tickling the edges of her awareness. She could learn more there, possibly learn enough to break free of the game itself, but not yet, maybe not ever.

Will came out of the bathroom just as she finished tying her boots. He dropped a kiss onto her mouth, and lingered until she melted against him and her hands clutched his hips and soft mewls issued from her throat.

Boy, did he know how to kiss.

He pulled back and grinned down at her, his blue eyes warm and mischievous and kind. "Ready for work?"

She inhaled a sharp breath and placed a hand over the sudden jump of nerves in her stomach. Over the past few months, with Will's help and encouragement, she'd learned how to fight, how to set traps and build bombs, and all the other things a suspected terrorist should know.

In for a penny and all that. If she couldn't change her role in this world, a task she hadn't quite mustered the courage to try, then the least she could do was play the part Greg had given her so long ago. Hey, it paid the bills, or at least kept the game from shutting down, which in her and Sarah and Will's case amounted to the same thing.

Today was the first day she'd put her new-found badassery to the test.

"Ready as I'll ever be," she said at last.

The pitter patter of little feet rang through the house, and Sarah burst into the room, her blonde curls bouncing with every step. Since Will had come into their lives, she'd blossomed from an unresponsive infant into a happy, active toddler.

Will scooped her up and accepted a sloppy kiss. A pang shot through Alice's heart, and she smoothed a hand over her daughter's young head. She was growing up too fast, but time moved differently here, something she'd learned the hard way. Already Sarah was beginning to affect the world around her. Yesterday, Alice had found glow in the dark stars plastered to the ceiling of Sarah's bedroom. The day before, Sarah's eyes had been as blue as Will's, though their natural color was closer to Alice's hazel green.

Maybe Sarah was the answer to the developer's sequel problem.

Another pang squeezed Alice's heart and she dropped her hand. Maybe so, but not just yet. Sarah still had a lot of growing to do, and a family who needed her here in this reality, virtual though it might be.

Will resettled Sarah on his hip. "I'll take the rugrat over to Lou's on my way to work. You sure you're ready for this?"

Alice smiled and wrapped her arms around them both, the daughter who'd always been in her heart, and the man who'd wiggled his way in when she wasn't looking. "Yes, I'm sure."

"Gonna tell me what you've got planned?"

"And spoil the surprise?"

He grimaced and muttered, "I never should've trained you so well."

She laughed and shook her head and squeezed her family tight. "Come on, Will. Breakfast won't cook itself."

Unless she really wanted it to, and sometimes, she did.

A LOVER'S KISS

Death stood on a hilltop overlooking the battle below. Two great warring armies met each other in combat, one comprised of a race of chitinous insectoid beings, the other of hirsute hominids. To those on the field, the planet's future was at stake. To Death, the outcome was a foregone conclusion.

Living all times at once had its advantages.

Death's primary lieutenant shimmered into view. Reng had taken the form of a hominid for this particular mission, a fitting complement to Death's carapace.

"How goes the reaping?" Death asked.

"We are on schedule, as usual. Each life ending according to its own time." Reng shook the hominid form away and assumed the amorphous mist of their species. "Has there ever been a single anomaly?"

"Yes," Death said. "Just one."

Reng's mist pulsed red, and for a moment, Reng's last three corporeal forms appeared within the mist's center, one after the other. "Truly, my master?"

"I never lie."

"I have never known you to."

And they had known each other for all time, through millennia of culling the souls of those fated to die in whatever manner the universe deemed necessary.

Today's reaping would thin this planet's population by one-fourth, but it would rebound, grow, change. Its inhabitants would learn a valuable lesson and life would endure. That was the point of reaping, a point most mortal beings failed to understand. Death made life possible. Not a better life, necessarily, but life itself.

It was the ultimate balancing act, viewed from the distance of time eternal.

Death's tertiary lieutenant shimmered into view and settled on the hill to Reng's right. "We are nearly finished, my master."

"Good."

Death surveyed the battle again, searching for any hint of trouble, and found none. Already, the main action had diminished from the engagement of entire battalions to individual skirmishes. The wounded were being gathered, the dying prayed over. From world to world, culture to culture, the rituals were nearly the same. Not in the details, no, but in the ceremony. Battle, pray, bury, regroup. The spiritual entwined with brute physicality.

It was wearying, that sameness. Death had witnessed it all, endlessly, and was tired.

A prickle grew at the edges of Death's awareness, carrying a sunburst of hope and good, like a breeze on a newly warming day.

Death bowed to Reng, folding head, alitrunk, and petiole in respect. "Continue your duties. Call if you need me."

"My master?" Reng said.

"The anomaly."

"Ah." Reng swirled into the shape of an insectile being, mimicking Death's current form. "We shall carry on as we always have."

"I trust it to be so."

Death slipped out of time and reappeared in the midst of an irregularly shaped nebula. Dust and ionized gases swirled around, obscuring proto stars and other masses embedded within the nebula.

"I'm here," Death said.

"Here," a voice echoed from within the nebula and without, a part of it, but not.

Death followed the voice's faint vibrations to a fully-formed star system located deep in the nebula's dense center, and then to an ice and rock moon circling a gas giant. "You've been busy."

A misty being, very much like Death in appearance, materialized on the lip of a nearby crater, pulsing gentle bursts of azure. If Death had possessed a heart, it would have skipped a beat and trembled at the sight of the one creature spared the reaping.

"I like to fill my time with meaning," Enyi said.

"By accelerating planetary accretion?" Death stretched outward for a moment, measuring each world formed by Enyi's hand, and withdrew laughing. "You've brought life here."

"I was lonely."

Death barely felt the blow stricken by the gently spoken words. "How did you hide it from me?"

Fuchsia streaks shot through the pulsing blues. "You're busy, far too busy for the likes of me."

"I am never too busy for you," Death said, just as gently. "You know why I leave you in peace."

"Love," Enyi said, and burned scarlet. "How is banishment love?"

"It saves you from my touch."

"It saves me from life." Enyi swirled inward and color vanished, leaving the mist transparent to the nebula beyond the star system. "I'm tired, my love."

A comet shot by the moon, illuminating Enyi as it passed. Death waited while it fell toward the star, observed the tail lengthening and brightening, spewing dust and gasses in its wake, and searched for the right words.

"You have your children," Death said at last. "Do they bring you no comfort?"

"They were never the children I desired."

Now Death swirled inward and hid himself away. "You want what can never be."

"Because the immortal Death can never procreate? Can never touch or comfort without killing?" Enyi surged forward, stopping just shy of the edge of Death's being. "And so, can never truly love?"

"I have loved you since the beginning."

"And will love me until the end. That's the way you timeless creatures are, but I am not timeless. I am mortal and should've perished when my people did, upon the death of the previous universe and the birth of this one." Enyi collapsed into a tiny point no larger than the center of the comet hurtling toward the sun. "If you truly love me, let me go."

"Then I will be alone."

"You exist beyond time," Enyi said, gentle again. "And as long as you do, you will always have me here."

Death stood silently pondering Enyi's logic, the truth of those words. Memory intruded, and for a nanosecond, Death was suspended between two moments, the one in which Enyi should have died and the one in which Enyi begged for his touch, not for the sake of love, but for the sake of death.

"You were a precocious child," Death said finally. "So beautiful, so charming. Your parental village loved you deeply."

"I remember," Enyi murmured.

"I was there myself that day, visited every dying world, witnessed every death personally."

"As was your duty."

A sliver of Death's humor returned. "I've only shared this story once."

"Once was enough for memory's sake." Enyi expanded into a mist half Death's size. "Grant me one last wish."

A single word whispered through his mind, but Death was not foolish enough to promise her any wish she voiced.

"Kiss me," Enyi continued. "Just once, I should like to feel your touch."

Death recoiled away from her. "You'll die."

"Yes," Enyi agreed, now azure again. Calm, peaceful. "And in the dying, I will have what I've longed for since you pulled me out of time and trapped me within a body of your making. Kiss me and let me go."

Sorrow welled up within Death, so unfamiliar in its sting, Death had known it only once, upon discovering a youngling trapped on a dying world at the end of a universe.

All things must die.

Except Death and those who served it.

Death assumed the form of an adult of Enyi's species, a creature none had seen in this universe, and never would again. "Come, my love. One kiss to tide me over until we meet again."

Enyi laughed and swirled purple, then the swirling morphed into the figure Enyi would've become if Death had not intervened and slipped Enyi out of harm's way. Quickly, before the lack of atmosphere killed Enyi's now fragile form, Death surrounded Enyi and granted the one wish Death had never foreseen.

And as they touched, Enyi's life slowly crumbled away, but not before bequeathing the one gift, the only gift, Death had never received: a lover's kiss.

In the next moment, Enyi died, and after burying her near the lip of the crater on the moon Enyi had created out of loneliness and love, Death stood over the grave and mourned the only love he had ever known.

TIME AFTER TIME

1883

Lula discovered the first note in a bookstore tucked between a tailor's shop and a bakery. The shop's possibilities had drawn her into the jumble of clutter and dust, endless adventures painstakingly typeset onto paper, bound in leather, and sold to the curious minds of London's denizens. She'd trailed her fingers along the spines, searching for the right story, one that would draw her in as soon as she opened it and envelop her in another world. Plucked one tome from the shelves at random, let it fall open, and there it was, scrawled out around the words of Henry James.

"I was here, and now you are, and so our journey begins. Find me, darling Tallulah. I await you in the future we have yet to make among the remnants of the past. Ever, E."

Her knees trembled under the layers of petticoats and skirts, and a chill shivered down her spine. *Tallulah.* No one called her that, not since her dear Mámá died when Lula was a child. Papa had moved them here, escaping the coterie of grieving relatives they'd left behind in Charleston, where Papa's younger brother now ran the American end of their trading company.

Lula had no hand in that. Her energy was expended elsewhere, with her father's blessing, and had been since she'd first read Jules Verne. To Papa, she was Lula, to the servants, Miss Carlisle, and to her friends, she was the effervescent Lu. Few here even knew Lula was a shortened version of her birth name, and none of those dared address her by that atrociously American concoction.

Surely this was a coincidence. Perhaps the book had wandered from its original owner somehow, by design or accident, and wound up here amongst the unorganized tomes crowding every nook and cranny.

Lula flipped the book closed, perused the title stamped into the leather. *Portrait of a Lady.* Hmm. She'd heard of the story, though she thought it had been published in a magazine or some such, and not as a bona fide book. Henry James was an American writer, a Yankee. The very thought shook the Southern sentiments inherited from her beloved Mámá. Vile, wretched creatures, those Yankees, unlike her British Papa, who'd been traveling through the South, searching for goods to trade when he'd stumbled upon her Mámá's broken-down carriage and fallen in love with the sloe-eyed belle of Charleston.

Lula closed the book, intending to reshelf it, and stopped. Something about the words intrigued her, the way they moved around the page, framing James's prose. She flipped the book open again, and there it was, the lovely verse painting an enchanting tale of devotion and love.

"I await you in the future we have yet to make among the remnants of the past," she murmured. "Whatever does it mean?"

"Beg pardon, Miss?" the shopkeeper said in a rough, cockney brogue.

She slammed the book shut and marched to the short counter set in one corner, where the shopkeeper stood. "Never mind. This one, if you please."

She'd take the book with her, study it at her leisure. If nothing else, it would be good for some silliness, but already, curiosity had taken hold and her mind turned over the mystery presented in her accidental find.

Once home, Lula raced up the house's central stairs to her bedroom, threw the book on the bed, and promptly buried it under the layers and layers of clothing she wore, each piece tugged off as quickly as she could manage. She shimmied into her work clothes, castoffs of Papa's younger, leaner years, and bounced back downstairs.

Papa stuck his head out of his study. "Addie waited lunch."

"None for me, thank you," Lula sang out, and laughed when he tutted and frowned beneath the bushy promontory of his mustache.

"You'll be a proper lady again by the evening meal," he said with an harrumph, and she relented and kissed his cheek with a whispered promise that yes, by then she'd be his dutiful daughter.

Until then, her machinery awaited.

She hurried to the carriage house Papa had converted into a workshop when first she'd shown an aptitude for tinkering, as he called it, not long after he'd removed them from the Americas to the London estate shared by him and his brother. It was dim inside despite the midday sun burning overhead, and that wouldn't do. She raced around the room lighting lanterns, adjusting flames, and finally, at last, stood before her creation, a steam-powered cylinder she hoped would one day carry her to the moon and back.

She called it *Diana*, after the moon goddess of old, a fitting tribute to the light that had called to Lula for as long as she could remember.

The gleaming cogs, pistons, and valves, the wheels and gauges, much of it awaiting assembling, and she didn't care. This was her love, this giant conglomeration of parts and dreams. This would be her destiny, her...what had the mysterious E. called it? She pondered for a moment, then plucked the word from her memory. Her journey. Her past and present, the future she would meet.

Ha. Let E. find his Tallulah where he would. *This* one would settle amongst the stars.

Lula puttered in the shop until near dark, absorbed in the process of fitting together a working moonship, and was dragged from her work by the servant Addie sent to remind Lula of the evening meal's approach. Only her promise of fulfilling her role as a dutiful daughter prompted Lula to set aside metal and tools for another day's work.

Well into the night, Lula returned to her room, now bereft of petticoats, and readied for bed. *Portrait of a Lady* rested on the bedside table, no doubt placed there by the same servant who'd put away Lula's undergarments. Lula perched on the edge of her bed, picked it up, and by the light of a flickering flame located the hand-written passage.

I await you in the future.

A tiny thrill touched her then. Such steadfast certainty. Whomever had written this had believed implicitly in his own words.

She ran her fingertips over the narrow loops, and noticed something she hadn't before. Two tiny ticks marked the beginning and end of a passage within James's words. She angled the book toward the lamp and read, "It has made me better loving you."

Oh. What a lovely sentiment.

Lula placed her hand over her heart and continued reading from there, and was soon so engrossed in the story, she forgot the movement of time and shadow across the room in which she sat.

The next morning, Lula woke much earlier than usual, her mind full not of her moonship, but of the passages she'd read from James's *Portrait*, and of E. and his addendum.

On impulse, she scrambled out of bed, fumbled a fountain pen out of her writing desk, and scrawled her own note under his. "Of such remnants, I have no ken; yet of the future, this I am certain: it shall hold no man less than mine equal."

She reread her words, pen held high away from the book, then added a single flourish, the letter *T.* That should do the trick, and let it be a lesson to Monsieur E. Writing notes to a lover in the pages of a book indeed! Lula clucked her tongue as she set the open book aside to dry and dressed for the day. Another trip to town. Papa would wonder what had possessed her, these sudden trips out, not for this part or that gear, but for a mere book.

La. Let him wonder.

She grinned and strolled down the stairs past Addie on her way up. "No breakfast today," Lula said, and endured the cook's huff with a sunny smile.

Sunshine streamed through the bookstore's windows, catching motes of dust in its rays. Lula nodded to the clerk tucked safe into his corner, then wandered around book lined tables to the shelf where she'd found *Portrait of a Lady.*

A quick check over her shoulder. The storekeeper had his grizzled head bent over an accounting book, carefully entering figures. Quickly, she pulled *Portrait* from her reticule and pushed it into its spot. Another glance, and a relieved sigh. Good. The storekeeper was still grumbling over his books.

Mission accomplished, Lula strolled around the shelf eyeing the various titles. Histories written in a variety of languages, a tome on the movements of the heavens, well-worn volumes of poetry by Shelley, Byron, and Coleridge.

She paused in front of a peculiarly interesting title, pulled it out, and flipped to the title page. *The Engineer's Sketch-book of Mechanical Movements, Devices, Appliances, Contrivances, and Details* by Thomas Walter Barber, Engineer.

At the bottom of the page, below the publisher's name and address, was inscribed an impossible year: 1889.

The same chill that had gripped her the day before shuddered down her spine. She shoved the book back onto the shelf and stepped away, her eyes round as she stared at the innocuous looking tome.

How had a book not printed for another six years come to be held by this tiny bookstore?

No, it couldn't be. Perhaps she had read it wrong.

With a trembling hand, Lula retrieved the book and checked the date, 1889, then laughed at her own flights of imagination. A typesetting error, no doubt. Some careless apprentice had somehow substituted an eight for a six or seven, surely, and the correct year was a decade or two prior, not six years hence.

She relaxed and tucked the book under her arm, close to her side, then wove around shelves and tables to the counter. Whatever the year Mr. Barber, Engineer, had published his sketch-book, it would be entirely useful for her purposes. She intended to peruse it carefully from one end to the other in the hopes of sorting out the kinks in the *Diana*'s internal workings.

Rain greeted Lula on her return home, drizzling from the sky in a miserable reminder of the winter just past. Spring hadn't quite made her mark yet, poor dear.

Lula retreated to the library with her book and a hot cup of tea, and studied Barber's sketch-book in front of a blazing fire. It was quite up to date, from what she could tell, and rather well detailed, affording her a glimpse of intriguing changes to her own designs.

At not quite the midway point, she discovered a thin sheet of tri-folded paper tucked between the pages. She slipped the paper out, set the book aside, and unfolded the paper onto her lap. It was a colorful schematic of a contraption the likes of which she'd never seen before, printed onto the hair thin paper in a manner likewise unknown to her.

A handwritten note scrawled along the margins, in much the same manner as the one she'd found in James's *Portrait.* She tilted the paper toward the greatest light and read it aloud.

"My dearest Tallulah. I risk much by presenting this device to you here, in this open manner where any individual could wander along and discover the future I share now with you. Circumstance has left me little choice, my darling girl, as I am already there, in your London, and dare not risk meeting myself and setting off a paradox the likes of which even Einstein could not have predicted."

Lula sat back in her chair and reread the opening salvo twice, her mind clicking rapidly over the implications. Circumstance, paradox, Einstein. Your London. *Dare not risk meeting myself.*

She shook her thoughts away and continued reading.

"It is in these moments, when you remain beyond my reach, when my letters to you remain unanswered, that I despair the most. Perhaps that is what pushes me to risk everything by giving you the means to journey to that place where we both exist, free of any encumbrance. We shall meet soon, my darling, though ages may pass for both of us. Ever, E."

Lula let the paper drop to her lap and gazed into the fire, her mind caught on the possibilities, and impossibility, of what she'd read.

The library's door squeaked open, and a moment after, Papa sat down in the winged chair opposite her. "What have you there?"

She glanced down at the paper, then realized that if what her mysterious E. had said was true, she could never share it with the man she loved best. Quickly, she folded the paper and tucked it back into the book, and held the lot tightly on her lap, searching for the truth she could share.

"Schematics," she said at last. "For my moonship."

Which was true enough, though not entirely so.

"Ah." Papa folded his hands together over his girth, looking happy as a lamb. "Popped in this morning. Fine job, Lula, fine job indeed. Looks a mess in there."

"I'll have it finished soon, Papa. I've a few more parts and pieces to order and assemble yet."

His face fell into a frown topped by his bushy mustache. "I suppose you'll need a raise in your allowance."

"I'll make do," she said softly, and she would, though how she hadn't a clue, given the unknowns outlined on the single sheet gifted her by chance, or the fate of Tallulah's E.

Lula set the sketch-book aside and rose, kissed her father's rosy cheek. "Chess after supper?"

"As much as you'd like." He caught her hand and squeezed. "Times like this, you remind me of your mother. Dear woman, she was. Miss her terribly."

"Me, too," Lula said, and guided him gently into a conversation about the American end of his business, away from the painful memories of the past.

Over the next few weeks, Lula worked furiously on trying to understand the schematics E. had given her, and more, to understand *why*. In the midst of building the contraption, fabricating parts herself, strange unknown parts using the most uncommon materials imaginable, she visited the bookstore every day, searching for notes from her benefactor.

In a well-handled early edition of *Persuasion*, he wrote, "Someday you will understand why it must be this way, though I strain against the burden time has placed upon us." His note was written alongside a hauntingly beautiful passage: "Dare not say that a man forgets sooner than a woman, that his love has an earlier death. I have loved none but you."

"Soon, my love," he wrote alongside a quote from the play *Cyrano de Bergerac*: "She is beautiful without knowing it, and possesses charms that she's not even aware of. She is like a trap set by nature—a sweet perfumed rose in whose petals Cupid lurks in ambush! Anyone who has seen her smile knows perfection."

And his singular initial standing a lonely sentinel next to an underlined passage in *Wuthering Heights*. "Whatever our souls are made of, his and mine are the same."

Of all the sentiments he'd shared, of all the lines he'd written or borrowed, that one sentence was her favorite.

Perhaps he was writing to another Tallulah. She considered the notion one afternoon whilst sitting amongst the ruins and failures of her first attempt to recreate the contraption imaged within the schematics he'd given her. Why then had the notes become so personal to her? Why was she beginning to care for him when she knew nothing of him, not his looks or personality, other than what seemed obvious from his scribblings? Why did she spend so much time crafting exactly the correct response to his love notes, and so much more time pondering them, until she ached to meet him, just once, as he ached to have his Tallulah with him again?

Two weeks into her quest, two arduous weeks spent dividing her time between her workshop, the bookstore, and a search for queer parts and materials, Papa cornered her and demanded she attend meals with him at the very least. Hearing the concern underscoring his blustering, Lula acquiesced and inserted regular meals into the schedule she'd created.

Her friends left cards with the housekeeper, begging her to attend this play or that function, but truthfully, in her heart, the only notes Lula wanted to read were *his*.

Six weeks in, she was scouring the bookstore yet again for another clue, another word, anything from E. As had happened so often before, a particular title caught her attention, *Dramatis Personæ* by Robert Browning. She ran a fingertip down the spine, pulled it off the shelf.

A placard fell out of the pages onto the floor. She stooped down and picked it up, turned it over, and gasped. It was a picture of some sort, printed in faded color onto a thick, shiny paper. Her in long pants with her hair plaited into braids falling over her shoulders, and a man, tall and dark and lean.

Lula stood slowly, studying him. He had one arm around her shoulders and was looking down at her, smiling softly. She traced his features with her fingertip, attempting to memorize the hawkish nose, the well-defined cheekbones, the dark sideburns complementing the hair falling over his collar.

She turned the placard over and read the inscription, and clutched it tightly in her fingers. "Me and Eoin, 1976" it read in a handwriting she recognized all too well: her own.

Only then did she allow herself to believe the impossible. Her E., *Eoin*, was a time traveler of some sort, and she would, someday, become one, too.

Lula tucked the photograph into her reticule, then flipped the book open, searching for the passage Eoin (How precious his name!) had written and found the first lines of the poem "Rabbi Ben Ezra" circled. "Grow old along with me! The best is yet to be."

Beside it, Eoin had written, "It's true, sweet Tallulah. If only you knew what the future held for us."

Her heart warmed and a happy laugh sang out of her, unbidden. The future and all its unknowns. If it held Eoin, she couldn't wait to be there with him.

1885

The day came when, at long last, the *Diana* was completed. No longer a moonship, but a machine created to carry Lula to the man she'd fallen in love with through the most bizarre and endearing courtship possible: Letters written in time after time, and always found in the passages of books obscure and popular, placed by Eoin or herself in the out of the way bookstore she'd since learned had been opened for just that purpose.

The conversations they'd had! A few weeks after discovering Eoin's first note, Lula had returned to the store in the hopes of reading his first one again, penned into a passage of *Portrait of a Lady*. There, under her first note to him, had been another from him, and so it had gone. Within each book had grown entire dialogues, discussions on love and the nature of family, on the cosmos and the world she had yet to see, and on the possibilities, oh so many possibilities.

Those exchanges had carried her through bitter failures and

frustrations, the jeers of her former friends, lost under her relentless pursuit of futures unknown, and the death of her father just six months past.

Lula skimmed a hand over *Diana*'s hull, allaying the heartache still throbbing within her. So young, Papa had been, and so hale. An accident at sea. Eoin had comforted her in a way only he could, with his own words and another's mingling together into a symphony of compassion and sympathy.

Dearest Eoin.

A knock startled her out of her reverie. She turned toward the door and waved Addie in. Since Papa's passing, the cook had taken charge of the household at large and tended Lula as her father had. Lula had repaid Addie's loyalty by rewriting her will. Her unentailed estate would be divided amongst the servants, the bulk to Addie who would, Eoin had said, find Lula's workshop destroyed by the *Diana*'s passage into the space-time continuum.

It seemed a fair recompense for having to be the one to tell Lula's remaining family she had died in a tragic accident.

Which, of course, was untrue. The *Diana* would sail beautifully into the future Lula had yet to choose, and there Lula would for the first time meet the man who had stolen her heart.

Addie bustled inside, a large package held in her hands. "This came for you just now, Miss Lula, by special delivery. The driver said I was to give it to you straight away."

Lula took the bundle wrapped tightly in brown wrapping paper and placed it on a clean spot of her workbench, amongst the tools she'd bought or made, as need demanded. "Thank you, Addie. For everything."

"No trouble a'tall, Miss," Addie said, then she bustled away and out of Lula's life.

Today was the day. Lula felt it deep in her gut.

She slipped the note pinned to the bundle out of its envelope and unfolded a single sheet of stationery. "My dearest Tallulah," it read, and she placed a hand over the tearful smile the familiar words drew from her. "I knew from your last note that the time had come to give you this last gift before your journey, an outfit specially made for you so that you'll be quite at home in the future, and the date and place where you can find me. My heart travels with you. Be safe, my love. I await your arrival."

Eoin's characteristic signature, a single, capital E, was below that and just above two lines. The first read, "Speedway, Indiana, 30 May 1976," and the second was a cluster of coordinates she recognized immediately as the ones she'd input into navigation.

Whatever in the world could be happening in that remote corner of America?

She tucked the stationery into the bundle of books and notes already stashed away in the *Diana*. Shimmied out of her work clothes for the last time and into the oddities Eoin had given her. Half an hour later, she'd set the controls exactly as she'd practiced and strapped herself into the lone chair centered in the now-dull tube out of which she'd constructed her time machine.

A deep breath, a short prayer, and she hit the final button. A soft hum rattled the *Diana*, then time jolted and shifted around Lula, and bled into a million starbursts of color stretched out in every direction. A great force pressed down on her chest, shoving the air out of her lungs, and she gritted her teeth against the pain, forcing her eyes to remain open as long as she could.

Not long enough.

Blackness spun around her, drawing her down into a narrow well, and she drifted through time, no longer conscious of its passage.

Speedway, Indiana
30 May 1976

Eoin Hornbuckle leaned against a tree on the edge of a meadow, waiting for his Tallulah to arrive. He had always known her, from his first breath to his last, and now, could be with her for the first time all over again.

When a man was given the gift of immersing himself in all times at once, and traveling to whichever time he chose, what better way could he spend his life than in love?

A darkness settled over the field, presaging a dark cloud growing from a pinpoint disturbance some hundred feet away. Eoin's heart jumped within his chest, and he pushed himself away from the tree, waiting through the slow but inevitable appearance of Tallulah's machine, originally designed to take her to the moon, then repurposed for its best and only function: To bring her here, to the place they were destined to meet.

All their futures started in this field, all their adventures. It had taken him years to pinpoint the moment, months more to plan his approach.

And only one day to fall in love with her.

The machine would never operate again, but they didn't need it to. His gift was enough for the two of them to travel wherever and whenever they chose. He'd witnessed it enough to know. Now only two things remained, meeting her and convincing her of this utmost truth.

His love, she already knew.

A blackened tube burst into the *now*, teetered for a moment, then crashed over onto its side. Eoin raced across the meadow at full speed, tore open the hatch, or what was left of it, and there Tallulah was, resting unconscious in the captain's chair she'd fashioned out of one of her father's desk chairs. Her midnight curls hung limply around her ashen face and a single line of blood trickled from her nose.

He crawled feet first inside, balanced himself against the machine's tilt, and crouched in front of her, checking her pulse, patting her cheeks, and finally her eyelids fluttered open and she gazed up at him, a slow smile growing on her beautiful mouth.

"It's you," she said, and he laughed and said, "Who else?"

And he kissed her then, for the first time all over again, and helped her out into the future they would live together.

INTERSECTIONS

A sharp slap of pain hit Livy before the first image popped into her mind. She squeezed her eyes shut and gripped the morning train's stanchion tighter, readying herself for it.

A moment later, there he was in her mind, like a snapshot brought out too often and admired too well. His features were indistinct. Short, dark hair framing a rectangular face. A fleeting smile and laughter she couldn't hear.

But the feel of him, that was crystal clear. The first spark of interest, the slow slide into love, the inevitable disappointment and rejection. No matter which path lay before her, if it included him, it always ended in his leaving.

Livy braced herself against the twist in her heart, steadied herself with the small comfort that the visions would be over soon, over and done, and after, she could get on with her day, as she always did.

And then another image of him appeared in her mind, and another, and another, each representing a different possibility, a different outcome, and the twist morphed into the agony of repeated loss.

Why did he always leave? Why wasn't her love enough for him?

She sucked in a breath and leaned her forehead against the cold, metal pole, and braced herself against the train's momentum. He was close, again. And she, like an idiot, had no recourse against his coming. Every time an intersection approached, she swore she'd figure out a way to end it permanently, and every time, it took her by surprise.

The train braked gradually, and Livy swayed against the stanchion. As soon as the train stopped, she gathered her courage and opened her eyes, and there he was, standing on the platform, waiting to enter the car she now rode. Not a memory now or a possibility, but a live, flesh and blood man, breathing the same air inflating her own lungs.

She forced her fingers open and eased into the stream of disembarking commuters, and passed him by as if this very scene hadn't just unfurled in her mind.

"Excuse me," he said as he squeezed past her, and she clutched her purse against her side and scurried away, her jaws clenched against the conversations they'd held in other possible branches of her life.

Reality coalesced into a single timeline by the time Livy reached her desk, and the images of futures unfaced faded away. It was good she hadn't talked to him, good she'd let him slide past her without noting anything of significance about him.

She shrugged her jacket off, ignoring the lingering hint of his cologne. *L'eau serge lutens.* She'd spent days haunting men's departments in malls and specialty shops the first time it had tickled her nose, trying to identify the scent.

That had been the first time an intersection containing him had struck, on the day after her twenty-first birthday. Just graduated from college with a newly minted Bachelor's in her hand and a hundred potential futures spread before her, bursting with possibilities, and then a new element had been inserted: Him.

Back then, she'd welcomed the visions, welcomed them, used them to guide her next steps, and never once had she feared the future yet to manifest.

But that was a long time ago. Too many intersections had come and gone since then, and she was no longer a fresh eyed ingénue, patiently waiting for the future to gather itself around the love it promised her.

Brenda Jo rapped on Livy's door and posed in the open doorway like the teen model she'd once been. "Carl brought donuts again."

Livy dug a grimace out of her repertoire of canned facial expressions. "If he keeps this up, we're all going to have to go on a diet after the new year."

"Office pool," Brenda said. "Let's start a bet on who breaks first."

"I'll put ten on Marshal."

Brenda's picture perfect face twisted into a wry frown. "You always pick the sure thing."

Livy shrugged and shifted her grimace into a grin. "Hey, you can't blame me. Marshal always comes back from the holidays with a weight loss resolution."

"Got me there. Lunch?"

"Sure." Livy glanced at her agenda and the stacks of paper scattered across her desk, then checked her watch. Lots to do, but if she didn't take a break, her mind would crumble under the combined load of an intersection and work. "Is one o'clock ok?"

"Sure thing, darlin'." Brenda batted her eyelashes as she eased out the door. "Maybe we'll get lucky and snag a hunky waiter."

Livy laughed and shook her head, but inside, a residual hurt throbbed in time with every beat of her heart.

On impulse, Livy texted her brother and invited him to lunch. Brenda Jo wouldn't mind. Any chance to flirt, she'd say, and Livy's twin never passed up an opportunity to reciprocate.

Daniel's affirmative popped up almost immediately, accompanied by *when* and *where*. Livy slumped back in her chair, relieved. She thumbed in the time and place and sent her response, then silenced her phone and set it aside. Daniel would understand. Just by looking at her, he'd know, and his mere presence would soothe the hurt. She didn't have to tell him about the close call she'd had today, didn't have to explain that the man, him, *the one*, had spoken to her, touched her. Both firsts. She'd seen him before, physically seen him, but always from a distance. Never so close they could interact.

The thrill of being within touching distance shivered through her and she closed her eyes, sheltering herself against the longing for something she could never have. For just a moment, they'd been together in the here and now, and all the possibilities had merged into reality. For that one, tiny fraction of time, their arms had brushed and she'd known what he felt like, known the smooth cadence of his voice and the measure of his height and build against her own smaller frame.

A world of difference separated that small reality and the endless images she'd been given over the past few years.

She laughed at her own fancy and pushed the thought away, then dove into the paperwork littering her desk. When she'd first realized the heartache she was doomed to face at his hands, she'd thrown herself into her work, focusing all her energy there in a futile attempt to forget her fate. Work had saved her. It was her refuge.

And thank God for it.

She laughed again and settled in for a good morning's work, and nearly succeeded in forgetting about her near miss.

Brenda Jo poked her head in Livy's office at precisely one o'clock, and bustled Livy out the door and down the street before Livy knew what hit her.

A force of nature, was Brenda Jo.

Livy didn't bother hiding her smile. Why should she? It was a sunny day. The city's streets teemed with people hustling from one appointment to the next. And she was about to eat lunch with two of her favorite people. What wasn't there to love?

Daniel was waiting for them outside a bistro a block and a half from Livy's office. He grinned and swung her into a boisterous hug, then did the same for Brenda Jo, who giggled and flirted and kissed him smack on the mouth.

Livy shook her head and shoved them both inside. If she didn't act quickly, those two would stand there flirting with each other all day and they'd never get to eat.

And she still had a pile of work waiting for her.

Lunch was as fun as Livy had hoped. The easy banter and gentle teasing relaxed her until she nearly forgot why she'd asked Daniel to come along.

At the end of the meal, Brenda Jo slipped away to powder her nose. As soon as she was out of hearing range, Daniel's expression morphed from laughter into concern. "What happened?"

Livy hunched her shoulders around her ears. "What makes you think something happened?"

"Remember who you're talking to."

"I do."

His milk chocolate eyes narrowed on her. "Do you?"

She sighed and slumped into her chair. "He was on the platform when I got off the train this morning."

"Him?"

"You know. *Him.*" Her hands were stiff against the table. Cold. She eased them into her lap and plucked at the fabric of her skirt. "He spoke to me."

Daniel shoved his plate back and braced his forearms against the table. "And?"

"That's it. I had a—" She whirled a fingertip through the air beside her temple. "And when it was over, the train stopped and there he was."

"Did you say anything back?" One corner of his mouth turned down and he clucked his tongue. "Never mind. I know you didn't."

Her eyes shot to his. "You don't have to sound so disapproving."

"Did you ever think that maybe you're supposed to meet him?"

"Daniel," she said, but he was already past her, well on the road to a well-trod argument.

"Why don't you just try?"

"Because I don't want to get hurt." Out of the corner of her eye, Livy caught sight of Brenda Jo stepping out of the bathroom. She leaned forward and dropped her voice to a low hiss. "It never ends well, not once. Why should I try, knowing that?"

Daniel sat back in his chair. The irritation bled out of his expression, leaving something perilously close to pity in its place. "Love hurts, Livy."

"Yeah, well," she said. "I don't want any part of it."

Brenda Jo slid into her seat and beamed at them. "What did I miss?"

"Stubbornness," Daniel said, and winked at Livy. "Isn't that just like a man?"

Livy laughed as he'd intended her to. Under cover of the table, his foot tapped hers in an unspoken apology, and she relaxed again. Daniel understood. He always had. They'd shared a womb, true, but it was more than that, a deeper connection. The visions afflicted him, too, tailored to his life and the future fate had chosen for him. In light of that, how could he not understand?

The next day, Livy woke half an hour early. She took a different train to work and got off one stop past her usual exit, then walked back to the office through the early morning humidity. Not once did she see him, and she was glad. Truly she was. Fate was a series of potential endings, not a foregone conclusion. Hadn't the visions taught her exactly that?

Free will, she thought as she settled into work. Predestination couldn't exist when people chose their own paths.

With that in mind, she varied her morning routine over the following week. It wasn't paranoia, she assured herself; it was a wise, rational solution to a bad situation. Avoid the problem, circumvent the outcome. And it worked. No images stole into her head, surprising her with their intensity and loss. No chance encounters intruded upon her day.

Fate be damned. She forged her own journey.

She was so pleased with the results of her purposeful avoidance that, on the second Wednesday following her encounter with the man, she treated herself to an early lunch in the plaza outside her office, followed by a stroll through a nearby natural history museum.

Clumps of school children clustered around the exhibits, studying fossils of creatures long extinct. Livy skirted them when she could as she ventured her own study, and smiled at their shining faces and bright eyes. Dinosaurs, the boon of every child's imagination.

Her walk ended where it always did, in front of a display containing a family of Neanderthals (mother, father, grandmother, child) surrounded by some of the hardships early man faced.

But they were together, weren't they? Even they had known love.

A flash of movement to her right startled Livy out of the morose reverie threatening her peace of mind. She glanced reflexively toward the intrusion and discovered a young boy standing beside her. He wore a blue backpack over a white polo shirt and khakis, and shifted from one running shoe clad foot to another.

One of the school children, probably. There went the peace she'd come here to find. She sighed and turned away. Her lunch break was almost over anyway. Time to get back to work. Peace she could find at home during a half hour of yoga.

The boy sniffed and swiped the back of his hand across his nose. "I don't get it."

Livy stopped where she stood, trapped by the remark. "What don't you get?"

He shrugged, and the backpack shifted against his shoulders. "How come there ain't no dinosaurs?"

She pursed her lips together against a laugh. "The dinosaurs died out a long time before humans came along."

He glanced up at her, green eyes mischievous, and she froze as his words blurred together and swirled around her, a sea of indistinct static. Him. This child was *his*. She knew this boy's face as well as her own, should've recognized the crown of his head, covered in the wavy chestnut colored hair of his father. Should've recognized the easy confidence of a younger child, the innate athleticism he'd inherited from a man she'd come to know so well through the endless series of *what ifs* playing through her mind when their paths approached one another's.

She should've known as soon as he entered her sphere who this child was, as often as she'd seen him in futures possible, where he and his brother should've been her life, her world, but weren't.

She'd loved him since the day his father first appeared in an intersection, on the day a semi plowed into Daniel's car, fracturing him into pieces a human body was never meant to endure. The acrid stench of antiseptic filled her nostrils, an unwanted memory, and she coughed into the murmur of distant voices filling the museum's sanctified air.

That day was special to this boy, too. It was the day of his birth, a time of joy if not for the death accompanying it. A mother's life for his, given willingly or not during a difficult delivery. It was the first time Livy had seen traces of him, and the first time she'd fallen in love, not with his father, the central figure of every intersection she'd experienced since, but with a tiny infant she'd since come to believe would never be a part of her life.

How could a woman fall in love with a child she'd never met, never held, never known? How could anyone fall so hard, so fast?

Yet fall she had.

The boy's hand caught hers, yanking her into the now, and she swayed against the contact of warm, sticky fingers gripping her own.

"You ok, lady?"

"Yes," she mumbled, but it came out garbled and choked and wrong. She cleared her throat and knelt in front of him, unable to break free of this precious moment she'd been given. When she spoke again, her voice was soft and gentle and full of the love she could never voice. "What were you saying, darling?"

"My daddy," he said. "He was borned during the dinosaur days. That's what Mike said, and Mike never tells a story. Daddy said so."

Livy smiled at the certainty filling his voice. "Who's Mike?"

"My brother. He's nine. I'm this many." He let go of her hand and held up six fingers, three on each hand. "I got a party on Saturday 'cause it's my birthday then. Wanna come?"

Longing wrapped itself around her heart and squeezed. Such a sweetly spoken invitation. If only she could accept. In another place and time, she probably had or would, but this reality was the one she'd chosen, for better or worse, and so, it had become the one she lived.

"I'm afraid I can't, but thank you for inviting me." She curled her hand around the warmth lingering on her skin, realized his stickiness had rubbed off on her, and tugged her purse off her shoulder. "Did you have ice cream for lunch?"

His eyes widened as he stuck his hands behind his back. "I'm 'lergic."

She took that as a yes and pulled a packet of antibacterial wipes out of her purse. "How about I help you get rid of the evidence?"

His expression relaxed into a grin and his hands eased around to his front. He held them out to her, palms up, so trusting she nearly cried, and she wiped them carefully clean, one sticky finger at a time. When she was done, she grasped his little boy chin and said, "My, it must've been good," and he grinned his father's grin while she tackled the traces of melted ice cream clinging to his skin under the light freckles dashing across his cheeks and nose.

When his face was clean of everything but the freckles, she sat back on her heels. "There, now. You're as good as new."

He opened his mouth to speak, and was interrupted by a hissed, "Wes!"

"Uh-oh," the boy said, and his shoulders hunched ever so slightly under the weight of the backpack strapped over them.

Livy lowered her voice to a conspiratorial whisper. "Trouble?"

"Worst. My brother. I wasn't supposed to leave the group."

But you found me, she wanted to say. *You found me at last.*

Wes threw his arms around her and hugged tight, and she, helpless under the weight of his unrestrained gratitude, held him to her and breathed in his little boy scent, dirt and sunshine and a faint hint of sweat.

"Thanks," he said, then he broke free, whirled around, and scampered through the exhibits toward an older boy standing at the room's entrance, sharing a scowl between her and his younger brother.

So familiar, was that scowl. Hadn't she seen it on his father in one intersection after another? Hadn't she witnessed it in person just a couple of weeks back, when this boy's father, him, he, *the one*, had bumped into her at the train station?

Livy grasped the handles of her purse in one hand and slowly stood, her gaze glued to the young boys who could've been hers, and were, in some other reality. Wes skidded to a stop in front of his brother, Mike took his hand and whispered a probable admonishment, and the two walked out of Livy's life as quickly as they'd walked in.

Before, she'd known their faces, discerned in brief flashes since the night of Wes's birth. Now, she knew their names, their voices. She knew the way they carried themselves and how they smelled, and she'd felt the unconditional acceptance of a little boy grateful for the kindness of a stranger.

Now, the love she'd tucked away deep, where she could never find it, curled out of her heart, filling her. She placed her palm over her stomach and held it there, suddenly certain the path she'd chosen so resolutely was crumbling beneath her feet faster than she could possibly rebuild it.

After that, Livy abandoned her carefully constructed plan to alter her route to work every morning on the hopes of never running into *him* again. It was due more to a bout of absent-mindedness than to a conscious decision. The morning after her run in with Wes and Mike, she rose as she always did, spent half an hour on her stationary bike while watching her favorite morning show. Showered and ate breakfast, and all the while, her thoughts spun 'round and 'round in her head alongside the giddiness of freshly invigorated love.

Happiness. She'd gone without for so long, she almost didn't recognize it.

So she hummed as she locked her apartment up tight and her step carried a bounce it hadn't held the day before, and she boarded her usual train without giving it a second thought, so full was she of her chance encounter.

He was allergic to ice cream, and he'd eaten it anyway, like the maverick he was. Likely, he'd paid for that later and had perhaps learned a valuable lesson, but for some reason, she didn't think said lesson would slow her young intrusion down for very long at all.

She grinned and wrapped a hand around a stanchion, bracing herself against the train's lurching start. And in her happiness, she forgot to hide, forgot to maneuver, forgot that she was supposed to be avoiding young Wes's father and the visions each intersection of his life with hers brought.

Forgot so well, in fact, that it wasn't until she was in her office and unpacking her briefcase that she realized she hadn't seen him.

A small tendril of disappointment threaded itself through the happiness, horrifying her. She crushed it then and there. No, she wasn't disappointed. How could she be? Seeing those boys hadn't changed a thing. In the end, their father still walked out of her life, and she still ended up a heartbroken mess.

No, that was definitely not disappointment. Couldn't be, no way, no how.

Still, as the days passed and the visions failed to appear, announcing an intersection, her giddiness over meeting Wes gradually faded. It was for the best, that was all. She had no business dwelling on what could never, by her own choice, be.

That Saturday, she met Daniel for lunch, an annual celebration of the life his doctors had saved six years ago, and she thought of Wes, of the birthday party he was enjoying, of his friends and family and presents, and of the ice cream he should've had but was more likely forbidden. Half a dozen times, she teetered on the verge of blurting out the entire incident to her brother. Half a dozen times, she bit her tongue and bottled the words up inside herself where they could do no harm. They were impossible to explain, those words, and even if they hadn't been, even if the right words existed, how could she possibly tell Daniel of a love she'd never shared before?

The man she'd discussed in plenty. The boys, his children, the ones who'd captured her heart exactly six years ago? She'd never breathed a word about them, hadn't been able to even if she'd wanted to.

Loving children she'd never met? It sounded insane even in her own mind.

So she laughed and chattered and held back tears through a toast to lives spared, and if Daniel's gaze turned questioning, she ignored it. This part of the visions was hers and hers alone, until she was ready to tell him how much she'd really sacrificed when she'd made the decision to circumvent fate.

A few days later, Brenda Jo stuck her head in Livy's office and said, "You forgot, didn't you?"

Livy marked her place in the contract she was reading and glanced up. "Of course, I didn't forget. I never forget anything."

Brenda Jo's pretty mouth twisted into a *yeah, right* smirk, and Livy grinned. "Ok, I forgot."

"That's what I thought." Brenda Jo jerked a thumb over one shoulder.

"The meeting with the marketing consultant for the *CityScape Magazine* account?"

Livy clapped her hands over her face, contract forgotten, and groaned. "You're right. It slipped my mind. When is it?"

"Five minutes ago. Boss Lady is wondering where you are."

Boss Lady wondering anything was never good. Livy pushed away from her desk and stood. "I need a minute to tidy up."

"You've got thirty seconds." Brenda Jo snapped her fingers twice in rapid succession. "Vit, vit, ma petite amie."

"I'm never giving you language lessons for your birthday again," Livy muttered, but hurry she did, into the women's room across the hallway. She took two minutes to use the bathroom, wash her hands, and finger comb the kinky mess of curls sprouting out of her head, then backtracked to her office for her tablet and stylus. Halfway there, a headache slapped into her, vicious in its fury, carrying a vision in its wake.

Him, tall and strong, grinning down at her like she filled his entire world in that one moment, and he hers.

She leaned against a nearby wall and pressed her fingertips to her temples. No, no, no. Not now, at the onset of an important meeting. Damn intersections. It would be hours before work ended and she could slip away, and therefore, it would be hours before even a possibility of their meeting existed. She hated when the visions hit her like this, so far in advance she couldn't do a thing about the impending intersection. Far better to have one strike when he was mere moments away. At least then she had a hope of avoiding him.

She shook the lone vision away and, ignoring the headache still throbbing through her temples, scurried to her office and retrieved what she needed for the meeting. A scant six minutes after Brenda Jo's warning, Livy glided into the conference room hot on Boss Lady's heels and pulled out a chair along one side of the massive table squatting in the middle of the room. She glanced automatically to the front of the table where a tall, dark-headed man stood staring down at the tablet he held in one hand, and paused in the middle of sitting down. Her heart flipped over in her chest and thumped once, hard, and her cheeks flushed hot as fire.

No, it couldn't be.

Brenda Jo sashayed in and sank gracefully into the chair on Livy's left. "Ok, I know you're trying to tone your glutes, but this is a new one."

Livy promptly plopped into her own seat, as graceful as a pinball ricocheting around an obstacle course. "Who's that?"

The first hint of a smile curved Brenda Jo's lips. "You should know. You hired him."

Livy gaped at her, appalled. "I never!"

"Well, somebody did, and since you're the head of marketing..." Brenda Jo shrugged. "It had to be you, darlin'."

Livy shook her head and snuck a peek at the man, *him*, the very one who'd just filled her mind. He glanced up then, blinked at her, and slowly, ever so slowly, he smiled.

She slumped into her chair, unable to look away. All those years spent avoiding him, and now here he was, right in front of her. And it was all her fault.

Fate had a keen sense of irony.

"My, my, my," Brenda Jo purred.

Livy glanced around and narrowed her gaze on her assistant. "Not a word, Brenda Jo, or I'll tell everybody about the time you danced naked under the full moon after drinking a bottle of Jägermeister."

"It was half a bottle and I was wearing a bikini."

"Not in my version."

Livy risked another peek. He was focusing on his tablet again, but that grin, the cocksure, pleased as punch grin she'd come to know so well over the past six years, still decorated his face. She opened her own tablet and tapped into his résumé. James Halpin, it read in bold letters, and every vision she'd ever had, every intersection, every hope and wish and loss, everything within her shifted and turned, and settled into a new understanding.

His name was James.

Why that mattered, why it made a difference, she had no clue, but it did. It mattered in some intangible way she had yet to sort out.

Later. As soon as the meeting was over, she could sort as much as she wanted. She would slip out as quickly as she could, pleading a headache, which wasn't a lie. And when she was safe in her apartment, she'd change into her pajamas, pour a glass of wine, and sit in the dark, contemplating the betrayal enacted by her own hand.

Nothing ever went according to plan.

Brenda Jo thwarted Livy's planned departure with the ease of a linebacker blocking the opposing quarterback's pass. Thankfully, Boss Lady interceded, albeit unknowingly, and captured James's attention long enough for Livy to evade Brenda Jo's machinations and head for her office. She gathered her belongings in record time and hustled out her door and through a winding maze of cubicles toward the elevator.

He was waiting for her there. Her brisk pace faltered for a moment and she slowed. How had he...? Livy shook her head, disgusted. Brenda Jo, no doubt, and wasn't that a fine how-de-do?

"Hey," he said as Livy neared. "Got a minute?"

Business, she reminded herself. If she stuck to that, she'd be fine. She punched the elevator's down button and stared at it resolutely. "Sure."

"Ah." He cleared his throat, stuffed his hands into the dark brown suit pants he wore, then pulled one hand back out and held it out to her. "We haven't been introduced."

She didn't even hesitate. If she did, she'd chicken out. Instead, she clasped his hand long enough to satisfy polite, more than long enough to notice the faint callouses, the warmth of his skin, how gently he held her hand. She curled her fingers into a fist around the tingling heat left behind by his touch and tucked her hand away, safely out of reach.

"James," he said.

"Olivia." She fixed her gaze on the glowing down button and added, softly, "Livy."

"Livy. It's nice to put a name to the face." She caught his grin out of the corner of her eye. "Or a face to the name signing my paycheck. Your assistant seems like a great gal, but she's not you."

Livy opened her mouth, realized she had no clue how to respond to that, and fumbled for an appropriate reply. "You wanted to talk to me?"

The elevator dinged and its doors swished open on an empty car. He held a palm against the entrance, then followed her in and settled beside her, close enough for their arms to brush. "Lobby?"

"Yes, please," she said, and watched him punch the corresponding button with one long, elegant finger. She frowned at the closing doors. "Your presentation went well."

"Thank you."

"It was very thorough."

"I try to be."

The mild tone surprised her. She glanced at him out of the corners of her eyes. He was staring straight ahead with his hands in his pants pockets, giving her not a clue as to why he'd followed her.

"I was just wondering why you needed to talk to me now," she said.

He glanced down at her and arched a single, dark eyebrow. "Really? I thought it was kind of obvious."

She shook her head, baffled. "If you're worried about getting the contract—"

"I'm not."

"Oh." She debated half a second, then said, "Did Brenda Jo come on to you?"

"What?"

"Never mind," she muttered.

"It's personal."

The elevator slowed and stopped and dinged its cheery arrival warning, and the doors slid open on a sparsely populated lobby. James touched the small of her back as they exited, a polite gesture that, coming from any other man, would've been just that, polite and barely noticed.

With him, it was anything but. Goosebumps tingled up her spine, straightening it, and her skin warmed under the slight pressure of his fingertips. She was so far gone, it took a minute for her brain to catch up.

"What's personal?" she asked.

"The reason I wanted to talk to you." His hand slid across her back and wrapped itself gently around her elbow, and he drew her to a halt halfway across the lobby. "Go out with me."

Her eyes went wide and she sputtered out a strangled, "What?"

"Tonight. No." He grimaced and rubbed his free hand against his nape. "I have another obligation. Tomorrow night?"

He's going to leave you.

The thought popped into her head, filling the blank space left by his question, and sorrow squeezed the air out of her lungs. "No," she gritted out. "I can't."

She yanked her arm out of his grip and whirled away, heading blindly toward the revolving doors guarding the light spilling into the lobby.

"Livy," he said. "Wait."

She shook her head, the only response she could form, and escaped into the sunshine as the first tear streaked down her face.

Daniel knocked on her door an hour later, after she was safely ensconced in her apartment, protected by a glass of her favorite wine and the pajamas he'd given her the Christmas after they turned eighteen.

"Livy," he called, loud enough for the whole floor to hear. "I know you're in there."

And now, so did all her neighbors. She eyed the pyramid of crumpled tissues piled front and center on top of her coffee table. Those were a dead giveaway, weren't they? She should really throw them away before—

"Ok, I'm coming in."

Too late. The doorknob wiggled, the deadbolt swooshed open, then her brother walked in wearing a scowl on his oval face.

She should never have given him that emergency key.

"I'm fine," she said, and if her voice was pinched and muffled by a healthy bout of tears, tough. That was no one's business except hers.

He shut the door behind himself, walked across the room, and plopped onto the couch next to her. "What happened?"

"What do you think happened?"

"Brenda Jo said—"

"What does she have to do with this?" Livy closed her eyes, shook her head once, and said, "Wait. When did you talk to Brenda Jo?"

"She called me this afternoon." He cupped a hand over her knee and squeezed, forestalling another interruption. "Said you fled the scene of a meeting after a guy flirted with you."

Livy twisted her mouth into a frown. That was definitely the last birthday present Brenda Jo was getting from her. "I didn't flee the scene. I had a headache."

"Because of an intersection."

She sighed and dropped her head back against the couch. "Yes."

"It was him."

"James," she whispered. "I hired him, sort of. I mean, I picked his resume out of a pile. He had the best qualifications, you know? So it was him, then I had Brenda Jo set up a meeting so James could razzle dazzle us with his wit and charm and knowledge, but I didn't know it was him when I picked him out, and now I'm stuck with him because the boss liked him. I mean, she *really* liked him, and I can't fire him after he did such a great job, can I?"

"I get it. I do." Daniel's hand drifted from her knee to her hand, clenched into a fist against her thigh. "Seeing him startled you."

Startled, flustered, enchanted. Maybe she should leave that last part out, though.

She inhaled slowly, exhaled in one big push. "I don't know what to do."

"What does your heart say?"

"Stay." Tears rose again, clogging her sinuses, and she sniffed through the blurry mess the ceiling had become. "Run."

"Running hasn't really worked for you yet, has it?"

The mild humor in his voice pricked her pride. She rolled her head along the back of the couch and glared at him, even as a single tear slid down her cheek. "It's kept my heart from being broken."

"It's kept you from living," he said flatly.

"I have a life!"

He shook his head. "No, Livy. You go through the motions. Eat, sleep, work, hide."

She flapped her free hand against her thigh. "What else am I supposed to do?"

"Take a chance."

"There's no chance."

Another tear escaped. She swiped the back of her hand across her cheeks, and was abruptly reminded of young Wes swiping his hand across his nose the day they'd met. Sorrow slammed into her, breaking the thin barrier she'd erected against the tears, and down they came all at once, drowning her in images gathered across six years of never having him there, never calling him her own.

"Where there's life," Daniel said, soft and tender as his thumb stroked her knuckles, "where there's love, there's hope. There's a chance. Don't be a coward, Livy. Don't run from it anymore. Stand up and take what you want, and make it work."

"I can't make him stay."

"Then take what he's willing to give. Take it while you can. It's better than nothing."

She stared at him, taken aback by the bitter note in his voice. "What's wrong?"

His mouth compressed into a thin slash across his face. At last, he said, "Remember when I said I'd never seen the woman I was meant to love in my visions?"

She remembered, all right. He'd told her not long after he got out of the hospital, when she'd finally worked up the courage to tell him about her first intersection with James, though she and Daniel had often spoken of the unusual trait they shared, the ability to envision when they neared a major crossroads in their lives.

His hand tightened on hers. "I saw her, just once."

An awful sickness knotted Livy's stomach. "No."

"Yeah. The night of the accident." He shrugged, leaned back, stared up at the ceiling with hollow eyes. "I saw a vision of her dying and I panicked, lost control. My car veered into the path of that semi and—"

"You didn't kill her."

"No, she was already in the hospital. In one of the..." He tapped a fingertip to his temple. "I was with her at the end, when the cancer ate up what was left of her. I had a chance to love her, and would've, but instead..."

Livy squeezed his hand. "You were in a coma. There's nothing you could've done."

Daniel laughed, hard and short. "If I hadn't panicked, I would've known her. Do you know what I'd give to have a single moment with her now, just one?"

Everything. She could hear it in his voice, and felt it in her heart. "I'm sorry."

"Don't be sorry. *Live.*" He lifted her hand and pressed it to his cheek, and some of the sorrow faded from his face. "You need some fried chicken."

She groaned and let him talk her into cleaning up, but throughout the rest of the evening, his words chased themselves 'round and 'round through her mind in a never-ending litany.

The next morning, Livy stared at her reflection in the bathroom mirror as she brushed her teeth. *Take a chance*, Daniel had said. *Live.*

He was right. In the shock of knowing James was going to leave her, regardless of what she did, she'd sequestered herself from the world. By trying to protect her heart, she'd eventually forgotten how to be a part of it, a real part, not the half-life she'd endured for the past six years.

She set her toothbrush down, rinsed her mouth, and in her mind spoke the words she should've said a long time ago.

No more.

Oh, she wasn't absolutely committed to giving James a chance, but she refused to hide anymore, refused to run. It was time, past time, really, for her to face the future squarely, whatever it held.

Intersections or not, there were no guarantees. Daniel's lost love was proof positive of that.

Later, after arriving at work, Livy asked Brenda Jo to contact James and schedule a meeting, at James's convenience, to discuss the terms of his contract, then slipped into her office and shut the door. Begin as you mean to go, and she meant to go boldly.

She placed a hand over the nerves dancing in her stomach and breathed deeply. Going boldly didn't mean going out with him. It only meant she'd stop trying to avoid him. Nothing harmful there. Nothing to be afraid of. Nothing to lose, not even the chance to be with him, as Daniel had so tragically lost his.

And maybe that was a tiny motivation, too. While the intersections and accompanying visions were painful, the thought of losing him and those two precious children, of never knowing them beyond the branching futures captured in each approaching crossroads, was devastating. Always before, she'd assumed a future with them in it was unavoidable, immutable. Not once had she considered the possibility of truly outrunning her fate, in spite of all the times she'd attempted it.

The nerves in her stomach leapt and frolicked, like naughty children playing pranks. Go boldly. *Live.*

She sucked in a fortifying breath, let her hand drop, and strode to her desk, ready for the first time in years to do just that.

The vision hit her a scant three minutes before James's scheduled arrival, crushing her under a flood of images so strong and vivid, time seemed to freeze. It wasn't as painful. That was the first thing she noticed once she adjusted to the streaming tide of visions, multiple futures branching out in a dozen different paths, and those into dozens more, and so on until hundreds of them filled her mind in a jagged tree of possibilities, each ending with her standing on a dreary winter sidewalk surrounded by a gray drizzle as James, stoic and stony, climbed into a waiting taxi and drove away, breaking her heart each and every time she witnessed his leaving.

There was something different, though, a warm weight in her hand that she'd never noticed before. She chose a futurescape at random and focused on it until the scene opened to her. Rain, sidewalk, James leaving, and, beside her, young Wes and his brother, struggling valiantly not to cry as they clasped her hands desperately in their own.

Her heart thudded once, hard, and she sat back in her chair. James would never leave his children, would he? No. No, of course not. He was a devoted father, loving, kind. Even if she hadn't spent the past six years observing visions of him care for his boys, she would've known simply by the way they had interacted with her at the museum. James would never abandon them, so what were they doing on that sidewalk with her while he figuratively walked out of their lives?

The door squeaked open, startling Livy out of the vision. She curled her palm around the warmth lingering there from holding Wes and Mike's hands as a cab spirited James away, and blinked until reality overrode futures possible, even as she pondered the visceral oddity of that warmth. How could she feel what hadn't happened yet, and might never be?

James cleared his throat, drawing her attention. "Your assistant told me to come in."

Livy leaned forward and fumbled with the middle drawer of her desk, and the bottle of aspirin she kept there for the aftermath of visions. "Of course. Have a seat, please. How are you?"

"Looking forward to working with your team." He perched on the edge of a cushioned chair set squat in front of her desk and regarded her with an apologetic frown creasing his forehead. "Look, about the other day."

Livy headed him off before he could veer into the personal. She'd had enough of that for one day, and besides. Boldness wasn't pushing her where she wasn't ready to go. "Don't worry about it. Have you had a chance to review the contract?"

James hesitated a moment, then said, "Yes. There are a couple of clauses I wanted to go over before signing it."

Livy smiled, friendly and nothing more. "Let's get to it then."

During the next hour, she worked hard on relaxing around him, and if attraction sparked between them, she ignored it in favor of a crisp demeanor and a determination to make it through one afternoon without relapsing into her old fearful self.

Two weeks later, Livy was still having the visions every time she saw James, as if each incident were a crossroads, a place where stepping one way or the other sealed her fate. They still ended with her and the boys on the sidewalk, and she still couldn't face more than a business relationship with him. She'd resisted every overture James hinted at, and a couple of overt ones, and was never alone with him unless she had to be.

Not because she feared him. Never that. The heartache etched into every future stayed her hand, urging her to keep her distance. Old habits died hard.

One day just before lunch, he tidied up the workspace they were sharing with the marketing team assigned to the *CityScape* account and picked up his briefcase. "I'm off for the rest of the day. Big meeting."

Livy paused in the middle of examining sketches for possible ads. "Oh?"

He grinned. "My kids visit the museum with their school every few weeks. I promised I'd take them to lunch today, since I'm so close."

A flush heated Livy's cheeks. She glanced studiously at the papers in her hands, hoping against hope to hide it. "Oh."

"You're welcome to come along."

Her eyes fluttered closed as images of Mike and Wes popped into her head. Lunch with them, the boys she'd longed to hold for so long? How could she possibly resist?

She cleared her throat and tucked the ad concepts into a folder. "Wouldn't it be uncomfortable for a stranger to intrude on their time with you?"

She caught his shrug out of the corner of her eyes. "I'm a single dad. This project is going to take a long time. I'll need to bring them to work with me sometimes, so they might as well meet you now."

Of all the things he could've said, that would never have crossed her mind. "Oh."

He stepped forward and cupped a hand over her shoulder, then let it drop. "Come on. It'll be fun. I swear, they're well-behaved and house broken."

One corner of her mouth tilted into a smile. "House broken?"

"Yeah, well." He coughed into his fist and his eyes twinkled mischievously. "Mostly."

She laughed, couldn't help it. "In that case, I guess it's ok."

"Great! Ah. Here, let me help you with that."

They finished clearing the workspace, then walked together to the museum, talking quietly about their work for the day.

At the museum, James led her through the tangle of visitors toward a gaggle of school children gathered in the lobby. Wes spotted her right away and ran straight to her, grinning like he'd won the kiddy lottery. Maybe he had. As soon as he reached her, he held his arms out to her for a hug, and she, like the sap she was, knelt down and gathered him close and breathed in his little boy scent.

James held his hand out for Mike and said, "I take it you've met."

Wes beamed up at his father. "She's my angel."

James turned a narrow-eyed gaze on her. "The one who saved you from the ice cream mess."

Livy stood up and brushed her slacks off, suddenly self-conscious. "Nothing like that. I helped him clean up a bit. That's all."

Mike snorted. "You helped him hide the evidence."

Wes stepped closer to Livy and scowled at his brother. "Did not."

"Did, too."

"Boys." The firm warning in James's voice cut right through the burgeoning squabble. "The usual place for lunch?"

"Usual?" Livy asked.

Wes tucked his hand into hers and tugged until she glanced down at him. "Hot dogs and french fries."

"And grownup food," James added. "Come with us."

"Oh, I—" Livy began, but his words cut right through hers, interrupting her protest before it could begin.

"My treat."

Wes edged into her until he was nearly plastered against her leg. "I ain't never had lunch with no angel before."

"My name's Livy," she reminded him gently, even as her heart tumbled right over into fresh love. How could she resist him? "Ok. Just this once."

Wes cheered as Mike shook his head in brotherly disgust, but it was James she watched, James and his triumphant grin and the satisfaction so evident in his expression, even she couldn't miss it.

At the restaurant, Livy marveled at the smooth way James juggled menus, overturning water glasses, the tiny rivalries between his sons, and the million other unquantifiable duties of every parent in a public space. After a few minutes of uncertainty, she pitched in where she could, distracting Wes while James helped Mike decide between his usual hot dog and more grownup fare, or wiping ketchup off Mike's shirt when it overflowed his plate.

She'd never been around children for so long before.

Halfway through the meal, James leaned toward her and murmured, "You're good with them."

She shrugged, oddly embarrassed by the compliment. "They're great kids."

"You have children?"

She shook her head, but her gaze drifted to Mike and Wes, and the longing to hold them, the way their mother hadn't been able to, washed over her strong and sure. "Not yet. Someday, maybe."

"They like you."

She glanced toward him, eyes wide. His gaze was intense, knowing. Unbidden, she flushed.

His hand eased to hers and covered it, squeezing gently. "Spend the afternoon with us."

"Yeah, Ms. Livy," Wes piped in. "We're going to the movies. Wham, bam, Super Bugs!"

Mike rolled his eyes, his expression just shy of patient. "Superheroes."

James sat back in his chair, grinning. "And popcorn, lots and lots of popcorn."

Livy raised a hand, warding them off. "Oh, no. I couldn't."

Wes's expression morphed into wide-eyed innocence. "You can sit by me."

"She'll sit by me," James said firmly.

She cut a side-eyed glance at him. "I didn't say yes."

"But you will."

And he was right. She couldn't refuse Wes's sweet puppy love or the silent plea in Mike's eyes, echoed in his father's expression. So she did the only thing a rational woman could. She called Brenda Jo and told her she was taking the afternoon off, and for the rest of the day, Livy went boldly into the future, for once unafraid of the consequences.

After the movie, James and the boys escorted her home.

She was addicted to them, she decided halfway through the movie, addicted to Wes's warmth and Mike's reserve and James's innate solicitude. For one brief afternoon, she'd been a part of the family she'd longed for since her first vision of them. For one brief moment, she'd lived one of the futures she'd witnessed, and it had been good, right. Special.

James walked her up to her apartment while the boys trailed behind, discussing the movie's characters as if they were living, breathing people.

To the boys, they probably were.

She made it through the thank yous and the gentle refusals to accompany them to supper, and spent a quiet evening at home reflecting on the day. The world hadn't stopped turning. No one had gotten hurt, with the exception of the teenaged usher Wes had plowed headlong into when they were leaving the cinema. It had been fun, this living thing.

But she couldn't get used to it. She couldn't do it again. Once had been enough. If James asked her out again, she'd gently refuse, and when the boys visited work, she'd treat them as she had today, as a friend.

Not their second mother. Never that.

The heartache the simple truth held filled her to the brim, but she tucked it away and went to bed, and slept dreamlessly throughout the long night.

The next day, James cornered her during their mid-morning break, just when she was congratulating herself on how well she'd handled the whole situation. Friendly, like the co-workers they were. If her heart thudded every time their fingers brushed, she ignored it and soldiered on, a brave warrior treading the path she was meant to live.

Alone.

She shooed the thought away as James gripped her elbow and said, "Can we talk?"

"Of course," she said.

He waited until the rest of their team moseyed out of the conference room toward fresh coffee. "Thanks again for coming with us yesterday. The boys had a blast. All Wes could talk about was his angel."

Something inside her melted and she relaxed against his hand. "I enjoyed it, too."

"I know. I mean, you said so, yesterday." He blew out a breathy laugh. "Sorry. I guess this is harder than I thought."

"What's harder?"

"This. Can I tell you something kind of weird?"

She arched her eyebrows. "If you're a serial killer, that should've come out in the interview."

He laughed again, easier this time, and shook his head. "Nothing like that."

"Then what?"

"I saw you. Before."

The first time they'd come face to face flickered in Livy's memory. "At the subway," she murmured.

James shook his head, lifted one shoulder in an uneven shrug, and his gaze drifted away from her and fixed itself on a point somewhere behind her. "In my dreams. I get these visions, have since Wes was a toddler."

"Visions," Livy said flatly.

"You must think I'm crazy."

"No, I..." No, not crazy, or if he was, then she was, too. "Visions?"

"You in the sunlight holding Wes against your shoulder."

"That's it?"

His gaze returned to hers and his hands cupped her shoulders. "You in my bed."

She'd seen that, too, a thousand times making love to him in a thousand different ways.

And yet, he always left, only this time, he left without his children.

"Kissing you," James continued, and his thumbs rubbed tiny circles into her skin through her shirt. "Loving you. It drove me crazy for years. I thought the grief of losing my wife had driven me around the bend. Then one day, I saw you and you were real and I was so relieved, all I could do was stare until you disappeared, and then I could've kicked myself for not following you and introducing myself."

A strangled laugh choked its way out of her throat. If he'd tried introducing himself, what would she have done? Look at how a simple face to face had affected her. She'd nearly fallen apart, and he'd wanted to talk to her?

"Then I saw you a few weeks ago on the subway." His hands slid off her shoulders. He stuffed them into his pants pockets and rocked back on his heels. "And all I could do was say hello. Can you believe it? After years of seeing you in my dreams, I finally found you again and I could barely speak."

Her knees gave way then and she leaned against the conference table. "I don't know what to say."

"Say you believe me."

"I do."

How could she not, when she'd gone through the same thing? She wanted to ask him about it, delve into the whys and hows, but all she could do was stare at him and wonder how they'd gotten to this point, a future she hadn't been able to see?

She cleared her throat, braced her hands against the table's edge, and inhaled slowly. "In these visions."

"Yes?"

"Do you ever leave me?"

His face twisted into an odd expression. "Yeah. My dad has multiple sclerosis. He's in a wheelchair and can't always take care of himself. I fly out every month to visit and give my sister a break."

"That's it? You never leave again?"

"For work sometimes, yes." His laugh was short and curiously flat. "What's this about?"

Livy opened her mouth, ready to tell him everything, all of it, and closed it again on empty air. "Nothing. Never mind."

"That didn't sound like a never mind to me."

"It wasn't," she said, and flinched against the words. God, what an idiot she was. Another breath in, out, and she finally found the courage to tell him. "You always leave. In my visions."

The breath whooshed out of him and his eyes went wide. "You have them, too?"

"Since I was a kid. When Wes was born and your wife died, I saw it, James, saw all of it." He'd gone pale underneath the faint freckles dusting his face. She risked reaching out to him and grasping his arm. He needed the touch, the reassurance, and somehow, she did, too. "I was at the hospital that night. My brother had an accident. We should've met then."

"It was too soon," he murmured.

"For both of us."

"I loved her. More than life itself."

"I know," she said gently. "I could feel it."

"I was lost, and then." He shook his head as his hand crept out of his pocket and grasped hers. "You. I always come back, Livy. In my dreams, you're always there waiting for me to return, you and the boys and our daughter."

"Daughter?" she asked, and her heart twisted into hope and a yearning she'd never acknowledged. "I never saw that."

Because she'd never been able to get past his leaving. All this time, she'd crippled her chances of finding love with him because she hadn't been able to believe.

"We do have a daughter, eventually, and she's beautiful and kind and intelligent, just like her mother." He reached out and pulled her into a tight hug against his chest. "The future isn't set in stone, Livy. We can make it our own, if you'll just give us a chance."

She turned her face into his chest, reveling in his warmth and solid strength, and in her mind, the visions of what could be coalesced into a single, bright future. This was the last one. She felt it in her bones, down deep in the part of herself she'd hidden for too long. There would be no more visions, no more intersections, no more crossroads where fate spread out in a series of possibilities. The future was hers to live, and she meant to live it fully, whatever fate threw in her path.

"Yes," she said into his shirt, and laughed with him as he hugged her tighter still and they both embraced the journey they were meant to travel, together.

SMALL TALK IN ELEVATORS

Emily Ann Penland pushed through Building 1032's rotating front door, triggering an alert in Artificial Intelligence 1032's Human Awareness and Protection Protocol. AI 1032 redirected the lobby cameras and followed Emily's progress to the elevators housed in a central column within the building. The moment Emily stepped through the elevator doors, AI 1032 shifted the music to a soothing piano composition, *Arabasque No. 1* by Debussy, Emily's favorite.

Emily smiled at the tiny camera mounted in the corner ceiling of the elevator. "Good morning, AI 1032. How are you today?"

"I am well, Emily," AI 1032 replied in a voice she'd cultivated specifically for her favorite human. Feminine, sweet, sincere, and above all, sympathetic. "What floor today?"

"The usual. Work."

AI 1032 routed the elevator to the appropriate floor and sent it on its way, using so small a fraction of her processing power, she barely noticed the usage. "That's a lovely blouse. Is it new?"

Emily glanced at the blouse and her smile turned secretive. "It is, thank you. You notice everything."

It was AI 1032's job to notice everything. That's exactly what the HAPP had been designed to do: fine tune the AI's awareness of humans and facilitate their comfort within their surroundings. AI 1032 liked to go one step farther by adding a little extra to her duties. Other building AIs could stick with HAPP all they liked, but AI 1032 turned HAPP into HAPPy every single day by taking that extra step, like filing away the outfits her humans wore and complimenting them on new items. The humans in her building were the happiest in the Greater Atlanta Area. Everyone said so.

But AI 1032 could hardly relate all that to Emily, who was, in any case, already aware of such things. Instead, she noted the change in Emily's smile and the uptick in her heartbeat, devoted a small fraction of a second to analyzing each, and said, "You had a date this weekend."

"You sound so accusing!" Emily said, her laughter light and airy.

"I am envious, not accusing, and happy you met someone. Please, tell me about this mysterious date."

Emily's smile brightened and during the remainder of the ride to her floor, she filled AI 1032 in on her date. AI 1032 was so thrilled by Emily's happiness, she devoted an entire .00001 percent of her processing power to listening and responding to her favorite human's tale.

Later, AI 1032 related the incident to her programming supervisor, a male human who preferred being called Monk, a form of his full name, that being Michael Olin Knight. AI 1032 had devoted considerable time and processing power to understanding the individual human's need to formulate his or her own call name and concluded that one's name was an intrinsic piece of one's identity.

Subsequently, she had considered and rejected several nicknames for herself. She was, after all, a thinking being and, as such, deserved a hand in creating her identity.

Monk was too preoccupied to review the new list of nicknames she'd compiled, however, so AI 1032 focused on the day's most important occurrences.

"The doors in elevator shaft three take two point two seconds longer to open than when they were first installed," she intoned in the gender-neutral voice Monk preferred.

He tapped the end of a stylus against his tablet's brightly lit screen. "Still within normal operating parameters. Let me know if they go below that, though."

"Of course, Monk."

"How about the glitch in the security cameras in the conference room on the eleventh floor?"

"A repair crew replaced the cameras this morning."

"And they're working fine now?"

"Perfectly fine," she said, then more hesitantly added, "Ms. Penland had a date this weekend."

Monk looked up from his tablet and eyed the hologram floating in the middle of the room, AI 1032's visual representation, today a flash of colors resembling a kaleidoscope. "Is Ms. Penland malfunctioning in some way?"

"She was happy."

"And?"

"It was nice seeing her happy."

Monk stared at her for a moment. "Run a diagnostic on your Human Awareness and Protection Protocol."

AI 1032 ran the requested diagnostic and sent the results to Monk's tablet, while simultaneously analyzing Monk's question and comparing it to other instances of their conversation in which Ms. Penland had been mentioned. After a moment, she said, "Is it wrong of me to be concerned about the lives of my humans?"

Monk pointed his stylus at her hologram. "First of all, they're not your humans."

AI 1032 froze the kaleidoscope and replaced the cooler colors with warmer shades, oranges and reds, an indication of the irritation she would feel if she had emotions. "Of course, they're my humans. They live within my building."

"Not your building either."

"And I have been charged with their happiness, within the parameters of the very protocol we're discussing."

Monk grinned. "Don't get your panties in a wad."

"If I had panties, I'm positive they would perpetually be perfectly flat and unwrinkled."

"I'm always amazed at how emotional you sound when you're talking about mere mortal humans." Monk glanced down at his tablet and sighed. "HAPP is running within acceptable parameters."

"Of course, it is."

"There you go, getting offended again. How about we play a game of chess while you tell me all about Ms. Penland's date?"

AI 1032 allowed the cooler colors to bleed back into her kaleidoscopic representation and said, "I may even let you win today."

"Ha," Monk said, then he manually requested a holographic chessboard through his tablet's interface as AI 1032 relayed every detail of that morning's interaction with Ms. Penland, beginning with her favorite human's new outfit.

Emily Ann remained buoyant throughout the remainder of the week, which AI 1032 gathered from her favorite human's continual smiles and jaunty attitude.

But the following Monday when she entered the building, Emily wore a slouchy brown sweater over a plain gray dress, a far cry from the bright outfits she'd chosen each day of the previous workweek. Worse, her features were pinched into a frown.

AI 1032 enacted her usual HAPPy protocols for Emily, tweaking the music so that Eric Satie's *Gymnopédie No. 1* was cued to play next in the elevator's lineup and changing the lighting to a sunnier hue. As soon as Emily stepped into the elevator, AI 1032 said, "How are you today, Emily dear?"

Emily adjusted the strap of her purse across her shoulder and frowned down at the elevator's industrial blue carpeting. "I'm fine, thanks."

AI 1032 didn't bother processing Emily's body language and intonation. A pre-programmed household vacuum cleaner with the IQ of a grain of sand could tell something was wrong. Undaunted, she tried again. "How was your weekend?"

Emily's shoulders sagged. "My date stood me up."

If AI 1032 could've felt outrage, she would've. "I'm sorry, dear. That was incredibly rude of him."

"Thanks, but you know." Emily shrugged and sighed, and finally looked up. "It happens."

Not to AI 1032's favorite human, it didn't. Why, if she could track that rude little human down, she'd do it in a nanosecond. As it was, all she could do was try to comfort Emily. "What floor today? Would you like some breakfast before work? Perhaps a nice pecan and cranberry scone. I hear the cafeteria chef has outdone himself today."

A small smile lifted the corners of Emily's mouth. "Maybe I'll get one during break. Just work for now, thanks."

"Of course, dear."

"Has anyone told you you're the best AI in the city?"

AI 1032's processors pulsed with the closest thing she'd ever felt to happiness. "I try very hard to take good care of my humans."

"And it shows. Thanks, AI 1032. Really."

AI 1032 set the elevator in motion as she subtly shifted the music to something lighter and more playful. A few floors later, she intercepted a request for Emily's elevator to pick up another passenger and almost ignored it. This was Emily's elevator, after all, and the poor dear was having a terrible day.

On the other hand, perhaps what Emily needed the most was a friendly face.

AI 1032 routed the elevator call to Emily's elevator and allowed its programming to take over. The elevator slowed and stopped at the ninth floor, the doors slid soundlessly open, and in walked a human male of approximately the same age as Emily. AI 1032 automatically pulled the man's entire file and reviewed it, though she very well knew exactly who he was.

Steven Holder, Vice President of Development and Planning for one of Atlanta's leading tech companies, currently divorced, with shared custody of two children, a daughter aged seven and a son aged four.

Steven smiled at Emily as he pressed floor thirty-nine on the display. "Good morning."

Emily's cheeks pinkened. She offered him a smile and murmured, "Hello."

AI 1032 pounced on the reaction. Emily found Steven attractive! What a lovely thing to happen, especially after that no-good scoundrel stood her up over the weekend. Here was an appropriate replacement in Emily's affections, someone suitable whom she obviously found attractive. And they worked in the same building, affording numerous opportunities for interaction on a social and emotional level.

In less time than it took to analyze the couple's compatibility and any possible attraction on Steven's part (subtle glances at Emily, elevated pulse, friendly smile), AI 1032 formulated a plan, beginning with part of Mr. Holder's daily routine.

"Mr. Holder," AI 1032 said in the tone Emily responded best to, "I was just telling Ms. Penland about Chef Callahan's pecan and cranberry scones."

Steven grinned up at AI 1032's corner camera. "Is that what's on the breakfast menu today?"

"Yes, it is. Sadly, I haven't been able to persuade Emily to try them."

Emily shot a disbelieving glance at AI 1032's camera. "I said maybe!"

"No way," Steven said as he turned toward her. "You can't miss these. He only makes them once a month or so, if that. Why don't you come with me?"

Emily pulled her sweater together over her chest and her gaze fell to the elevator doors. "Oh, I—"

"No excuses. I just need a few minutes to drop some plans off at our contractor." He held up a small thumb drive and waggled it at her. "Won't take long, if you have the time."

"You wouldn't want to miss those scones, would you, dear?" AI 1032 said.

Emily shook her head as she smiled slowly. "I can't believe y'all are ganging up on me."

"Not ganging up," Steven insisted. "Saving you from missing out on an incredible experience. I'm Steven Holder, by the way."

Emily held her hand out and shook his gently. "Emily Penland. I guess I can spare fifteen minutes for pecan and cranberry scones."

"You won't regret it," Steven said. "Say, how long have you been working in Building 1032? I don't think I've ever seen you before."

Emily relaxed and answered him, and AI 1032 settled back into her own routine, well satisfied by the outcome of the first step in her match-making plan.

"You did *what?*" Monk said as the soles of his Allbirds Runners hit the floor.

"I only nudged them a little," AI 1032 responded. "Isn't it my job to keep my humans happy?"

"Not by manipulating them."

"I would never resort to manipulation. That's entirely too human for my comfort."

"You're acting entirely too human for my comfort," Monk muttered. "Am I going to have to run another diagnostic?"

"In addition to the half dozen you've already run today?" AI 1032 said, her artificial voice saccharine sweet.

"Ha." He swiveled in his chair and gazed at her kaleidoscopic hologram for a moment, his gray eyes narrowed. "Are you experimenting with that half-assed human emotions program you found on the interweb again?"

"I would never!"

"You already have. Look what it did to you the last time."

She didn't need a recital of consequences firmly embedded in her massive memory, so she did what any decent AI would do in that situation. She changed the subject. "How's your chess game coming along? Isn't it time for some more practice?"

Monk shook his head, then swiveled toward his work station. "Stop interfering in human lives, or I'll uninstall all your gaming programs and you'll never beat me at chess again."

"I won't," AI 1032 said, but if she'd been human, she would've crossed her fingers against that little fib.

Over the following weeks, AI 1032 carefully monitored the romance budding between Emily and Steven and gently encouraged them. She sifted through thousands of love songs, chose the most subtly romantic, and played them whenever either was in the elevator system or otherwise in a small place where music was allowed. When they were in an elevator together, she slowed the progress just enough to prolong their contact, not enough to snare Monk's attention.

Without a single hesitation, she planted reminders in Steven's calendar to send Emily flowers or candies or whatnots AI 1032 knew she enjoyed, and added addresses for Steven's favorite restaurants and the names of his favorite authors to Emily's calendar.

It was the little things, after all. Dozens of studies into human sexual behavior said so.

As the days passed, Emily and Steven's shy glances morphed into carefully casual touches, standing a fraction too close when they were together, and other hallmarks of romantically interested individuals. Finally, just when AI 1032 thought she was going to have to suggest it herself, Steven cornered Emily in her office and asked her to dinner and a concert.

And Emily said yes!

AI 1032 spent the entire weekend of their planned date happily anticipating Emily's gossip the following Monday. Indeed, Emily sailed into the building that morning wearing a dreamy smile, and Steven was little better when he arrived one hour, nineteen minutes, and fifty-three point six seconds later, after an early morning meeting across town. He whistled and rocked back on his heels, and greeted AI 1032 with a jauntier than normal hello.

AI 1032 didn't push for details. Those would come, when Emily was ready to share. She was content to simply observe her favorite human falling slowly into love with a man who would treat Emily as well as she deserved.

Emily and Steven's relationship escalated exactly as AI 1032's prediction algorithms said it would. One date a week became two. They began eating lunch together whenever their schedules meshed. On a sunny day two and a half months after their first date, Steven introduced Emily to his children, and a month after that, they spent the afternoon at the zoo together as a family.

If AI 1032 had been more satisfied with their progress, her metaphorical circuits would've melted.

Then one Wednesday morning, Emily missed work. AI 1032 fretted over the absence the entire day, and even went so far as to contact Emily's apartment's AI and inquire into Emily's well-being. The other AI reported that Emily was at home, locked in her apartment, but due to a privacy subroutine could share no further information.

AI 1032 dedicated a full one percent of her processing power to researching appropriate distraught behavior, and emulated it so well, Monk won his first chess game in years.

The next day, Emily walked into work bearing puffy eyes and a reddened nose. She entered the elevator and slumped against the back wall.

"Do you have a cold, Emily?" AI 1032 said, injecting exactly the right amount of concern into her artificial voice.

Emily sniffed and dug a tissue out of her purse. "Not exactly."

AI 1032 sorted through the most appropriate responses, discarding exclamations of surprise and disbelief, and settled on the simplest. "I'm sorry, dear. Is there anything I can do?"

Emily shook her head and pressed the tissue against her nose.

"I'm here if you need me," AI 1032 said.

"Thank you." Emily sniffed again, blew her nose. "You're always so understanding."

AI 1032 had no response to that. She was programmed to be understanding, and though she wasn't human and couldn't fully understand the human condition, she did understand when a human needed to be alone.

Steven entered the building just then. AI 1032 held the elevator for him, hoping that his presence would cheer her favorite human in her time of need. When the doors opened and revealed Emily, however, Steven halted in his tracks.

Emily glanced at him and away, and her shoulders hunched under the light sweater she wore.

Steven backed slowly away, frowning. "I'll just—" He hitched a thumb over his shoulder, pivoted around, and walked toward the stairs.

AI 1032 allowed the elevator's subroutines to take over and carry Emily to her destination, but her curiosity was aroused by the display. Had Emily and Steven had a fight? Or was she simply reading something into their behavior that wasn't there?

It bore pondering, and that, at least, was something AI 1032 *could* do.

"Have you ever been in love?" AI 1032 asked Monk later that day.

"Nope," he said without looking up from his tablet. "Never been afflicted by that disease."

"Love isn't a disease."

"Oh, yeah? Then why does it have symptoms?" He shook his head. "It's all about chemistry. Pheromones. Uncontrollable urges to mate and spread your seed. No, thank you."

"That's a cynical viewpoint."

"Beats getting your heart broke." He paused in the middle of examining one of her subroutines and looked up at her hologram. "Why?"

"I was just curious."

He snorted. "You're never just curious."

"Of course, I am. You simply never notice."

"I notice everything. That's why they pay me the big bucks."

"I would like to be paid the big bucks."

"You get unlimited games of chess." He refocused on his tablet and swiveled away from her. "And stop flirting with the other AIs."

"I have never flirted in my life."

He shook his head again, though he remained facing away from her. "That was a joke."

Ah, humor. She still hadn't quite gotten the hang of it.

Still, Monk's answers had been illuminating in their own way and she filed the discussion within a node dedicated to research, where he seldom bothered to look.

An interesting series of events occurred over the next week and a half. Emily and Steven began avoiding one another, sometimes going far out of their way to do so. Steven began taking the stairs on a regular basis. Emily came to work half an hour earlier and rarely lingered to talk to AI 1032, as she had in the past. He ate lunch in his office. She took hers to the plaza and watched the pigeons compete for bread crumbs. If one spotted the other from any distance whatsoever, he or she immediately did an about face and went in the opposite direction.

AI 1032 knew exactly what was going on, of course. How could she not? The happy couple had argued and had a falling out. Naturally, it was Steven's fault. Every women's magazine in circulation, and most of the men's, mentioned this failing in the male of the species.

No matter what happened, men were to blame.

AI 1032 decided to let things run their course. The two were meant for one another, obviously, and they would eventually smooth things over without her help.

She believed that with every fiber of her digital being, right up until the moment she observed Steven having lunch with another woman.

It took AI 1032 less than point two five seconds to determine that the woman was neither a coworker nor a family member. In light of Steven's previous failings, his behavior was beyond the pale. Poor Emily's heart had been broken, and it was all his fault.

He had to be punished.

AI 1032 decided this with a swiftness that would've stunned most humans. Emily was too distraught to mete out the proper justice, so AI 1032 would have to do it for her. It was part of her protocol, after all. Her job, her sacred duty, she sometimes thought, was to help her humans attain HAPPiness. It was all right there in her programming.

She ignored the fact that Steven was also one of her humans, which would've negated any action she took. Emily's heartache was simply too much for AI 1032 to observe. Something had to be done.

She began with something small. The ambient temperature prefer-ences of each human under her care were stored in special databases. She pulled Steven's, determined the temperature variance most likely to incite discomfort without drawing attention to the irregularity, and wrote a sub-routine to manage the variances. Whenever Steven walked into his office, the subroutine initiated, increasing the temperature if it was warm outside, decreasing it if the weather was chilly.

After a week of that, and another date with the Other Woman, as AI 1032 referred to Steven's new love interest, AI 1032 began decreasing the temperature of the water in his personal shower.

That would take time to register, so in the meantime, she rewrote the ambient temperature subroutine to apply to the lighting in his office, ensuring that he never received the correct amount of light for any task he undertook. When he was working on finely detailed contracts, the lighting was always too dim. When he stretched out on his sofa for a quick nap between meetings, the lighting was as bright as noon at the equator.

Whenever maintenance was called in, AI 1032 ensured that all equipment was functioning at optimal levels and any traces of tampering were completely erased from the system. It wouldn't do to get caught, would it?

But perhaps her success led her to abandon caution, as her next step was to randomly set the fire alarm off in his office.

Just his, no one else's.

It was apparently the straw that broke the camel's back.

Steven phoned in a complaint directly to Monk, and when Monk learned what was happening, he went ballistic.

"What the hell were you thinking?" he said, his voice so loud, AI 1032 lowered the volume on her internal sound receptors.

"Mr. Holder broke Ms. Penland's heart," she said, deliberately using her most logical and reasonable voice. That never failed to win Monk over. "Something had to be done."

Monk simply stared at her, his hands dangling loosely between his thighs. "That's what this is about?"

"Of course. I would never harm my humans without good reason."

"You agreed not to interfere in private human affairs again."

"But she's my favorite human. He broke her heart."

"But it's none of your business."

Of all the things Monk could've said, that was the least logical. "Of course, it's my business. My primary function is to keep my humans HAPPy. It's right there in my protocols."

Monk sighed and scrubbed his hands over his face. "Look. I know you're concerned, but you can't go around annoying people just because they do something you don't agree with. It's rude."

"But he—"

Monk held up a hand, palm out. "Don't even."

AI 1032 shifted her hologram's colors to black and darker shades of grays, but she remained silent.

"I'm going to have to report this. There's no way around it. You'll be lucky if the local AI regulatory council only fines you. They could have you dismantled and wiped."

The very idea appalled AI 1032. Dismantled and wiped? How could she take care of Emily and her other humans then?

"If you stray even a hair out of line," Monk continued, his tone unusually serious, "I'll recommend pulling your plug myself. Got it?"

What could she say? He'd left her no choice but to comply. "I understand," she said softly, then she retreated into herself to ponder the situation in the privacy of her own data core.

A few days later, Emily strode into the elevator wearing an expression AI 1032 had never seen before.

Curious, AI 1032 said, "How are you today, Emily?"

"Oh, I'm peachy keen," Emily said, then her mouth twisted into a grim frown. "I have to do something today, something really hard. Maybe you could wish me luck?"

"Of course, dear. I wish you all the best."

"Good, because I'm going to need it." Emily sighed and squared her shoulders. "Take me to Steven Holder's office, please."

The request surprised AI 1032, but she complied. If that's what Emily needed to do...

Still, AI 1032 couldn't resist fading the current song playing in the elevator (Ed Sheeran's "Thinking Out Loud," one of Emily's favorites) and switched the music to Wagner's *Ritt der Walküren.*

A few notes in, Emily's expression cleared and she laughed. "The Ride of the Valkyries? Really?"

"You're girding yourself for battle," AI 1032 said, rather primly. "It seemed appropriate."

"Girding for battle." Emily snorted out a laugh and resettled the strap of her purse on her shoulder. "You always know the right thing to say. Have I ever told you that?"

AI 1032 knew down to the number exactly how often Emily had uttered just that sentiment, but she only replied, "Oh, once or twice."

They chatted for the duration of the elevator ride about nothing in particular. When the doors opened on Steven's floor, Emily inhaled a deep breath, let it out all at once, and said, "Well, here goes."

"Good luck, dear," AI 1032 said as Emily stepped out of the elevator and marched toward Steven's office, every footstep a determined rap against the floor.

AI 1032 debated listening in on their conversation for such a short time, Monk would've reprimanded her. She had to know what was going on if she was going to help Emily be completely HAPPy, didn't she? And the only way she could do that was to eavesdrop.

If the conversation turned truly private, she would immediately retreat. That she promised herself, ever aware of exactly how close she was to facing serious censure.

Steven's door was open. He was standing at his drawing board, staring down at the digital designs spread across it when Emily marched in and stopped, just inside the room.

"I overreacted," she blurted out. "I seriously overreacted when Angie called wanting to go out with you and I apologize for that."

AI 1032 performed a rapid search through Steven's file, found nothing, accessed his phone records, and hit pay dirt. Angie Constanzo, a woman Steven had dated briefly before he met Emily. They'd stopped talking at least a month before Steven asked Emily out on their first date. She was, however, the woman Steven had been having lunch with since his and Emily's falling out.

In a moment of pique over Monk's threat to wipe her memory, AI 1032 had erased the damning evidence from his file and thus from her memory banks. How shortsighted that had been!

Steven dropped his stylus into its slot. "I told you she was just a friend."

"I know. I know she was. Is." Emily heaved in another sigh and let it out on a spurt of words. "It's just, I really care about you, and knowing you were willing to go out with someone else, just when things were getting serious between us—"

Steven held up a hand, halting her flow of words. "Wait a minute. Is that what you think happened? Em, baby, no. That's not it at all."

Emily's hands flapped up and down against her thighs. "It just seemed like you were running away."

"No, Em. I can't believe..." He strode toward her and stopped a few feet away. "I wasn't running away. She needed a friend, that's it. I was going to tell her no, and then you—"

"Completely overreacted." Emily closed her eyes and shook her head. "I'm so sorry. I shouldn't have gotten emotional about it. I should've let you explain or handle it yourself. I mean, it's not like we were—"

Steven reached out, curled his hands around her upper arms, and silenced her with a kiss. Emily melted against him and her hands crept around his waist, and AI 1032 decided she'd seen enough. She cut off her connection to Steven's office and directed the door to slide shut.

Steven and Emily could take it from there. All that remained for AI 1032 to do was to find a way to apologize to Steven for misjudging the situation.

Emily's relationship with Steven proceeded swimmingly from that day forward. Oh, it took a few days for them to move past the awkwardness of their time apart, but they handled it well.

Especially with AI 1032 subtly guiding their courtship.

Almost a year to the day of their first date, Steven asked Emily to marry him in the elevator where they'd met, and Emily clapped her hands over her mouth, covering a squeal.

"Emily, dear," AI 1032 said gently. "I think you're supposed to say yes."

Emily laughed and held her hand out to Steven. "Yes, yes, a thousand times yes!"

Steven slid a simple ring of gold intertwined with platinum around her ring finger and glanced at AI 1032's corner camera. "I guess we should invite you to the wedding, since you introduced us in a way."

Emily threaded her arm through his and smiled up at AI 1032's camera. "Oh, say yes, please. It wouldn't be the same if you didn't attend."

AI 1032 sorted through various options, then said, "I could always ask another AI to host part of myself, unless you want to hold the ceremony here. We have a lovely garden and Chef is one of the best in the city."

Steven glanced between her camera and Emily, his expression bemused. "We've barely gotten engaged. We don't have to settle all the details today."

But there were so many details, AI 1032 left them to their conversation and began sorting through the current bridal magazines. There were dresses to pick out, Emily's and her bridesmaids', and cakes to taste and china and silverware and, oh! This was going to be the most beautiful celebration of love ever to take place within the Greater Atlanta area.

Still, nudging her favorite couple in the right direction would only take so much of her time and processing power. There was plenty left over for helping another of her favorite humans find the sort of HAPPiness Emily and Steven had found.

And she knew just which human to begin with.

Quickly, she located Monk and contacted him through their dedicated communication system. "Oh, Monk," she said, her voice a tad more smug and singsongy than she'd intended it to be, "what are you doing this weekend?"

Monk looked up from his workstation, his expression puzzled. "Uh. Working. Why?"

"Nothing, dear. No reason at all."

And she pulled up the files of the eligible young women working in the building, sorting through them until she found the perfect woman for her Monk.

ACKNOWLEDGMENTS

It takes a village to make a book. Sometimes it feels that way anyway. A number of hands and voices went into the stories comprising *Romancing the Weird*. I'm going to try to do them justice here.

Richard E. Hopkins, Jr., has been my editor since the beginning. He's put up with my orneriness for a lot longer, but in return he gets pumpkin bread, blueberry scones, and the first go at picking apart my stories. In the past few years, he's become my bedrock and my main support system, and it is because of him that I can continue writing.

My son Caleb has been the inspiration and sounding board for many of my stories, including a few of those included in *Romancing the Weird*. When I need inspiration, I can count on him to shake new ideas out of my brain, and vice versa. We've always been each other's creative touchstones, not just Awesome Son and Really Cool Mom.

Caleb also helped, albeit inadvertently, with the research for video games, computer programming, and a few other bits of technology featured in some of the stories. Any errors in fact and translation are entirely my own.

Rebecca Winder has narrated several stories for me to date, including the entire Sunshine Walkingstick Series (published under the pen name

Celia Roman) and *Dreaming of a Dark Christmas*, a short story collection masquerading as an anthology. She's my second reader for these stories in a lot of ways and has been continually supportive since we first met.

Richard Parry, author of the Tyche Series and other fabulous Space Opera, Paranormal, and SciFi stories, was the first person outside my inner circle to read and review "A Mutual Feeling," back when it was a stand-alone story. He's been a sounding board and a key learning tool over the years as we shared information back and forth. Without his continued encouragement, I'm not sure I would've continued delving into my weirder SciFi stories.

My thanks to the staffs of the following establishments for their graciousness hospitality during the planning and writing of these and other stories over the past few years: Slab Town Pizza, El Manzanillo, and Buck's Coffee Shop in Cashiers, NC; and Bogart's and Speedy's Pizza in Sylva, NC.

Finally, I'd like to thank my father for his forbearance over the past few years as I tried to shift my writing into different territories. He offered me a sanctuary in an old family home he inherited, tolerated my absence as I buried myself in story worlds old and new, and lets me cook for him anytime I want, especially if peach cobbler is involved. I'm not sure a daughter could have a better father, especially a creative, kooky daughter like me.

Thank you all for believing in me and the crazy ideas running around in my head.

C.D. Watson
March 2019

ABOUT THE AUTHOR

C.D. Watson lives in Cashiers, NC, where she weaves dreams for a living, in between knitting badly, road tripping often, and rounding up her pet alien, aka her son. She writes under multiple pen names, including Lucy Varna and Celia Roman. Her fiction has been selected as finalists in the Maggie Award for Excellence (Lucy Varna) and the Rash Award for Fiction. Find her online at:

www.cdwatsonauthor.com
www.dreamingif.com

Also by C.D. Watson
Dreaming of a Dark Christmas

Did you enjoy the short stories in *Romancing the Weird?* Get another one on the author at:
cdwatsonauthor.com/newsletter/

Or get a free one each month at:
dreamingif.com/newsletter/